ROUNDTABLE REDCAP

ROUNDTABLE REDCAP

PROVIDENCE PARANORMAL COLLEGE BOOK SIX

D.R. PERRY

LMBPN Publishing
PMB 196, 2540 South Maryland Pkwy
Las Vegas, NV 89109

Version 2.0 June, 2021
ebook ISBN: 978-1-64971-831-0
Print ISBN: 978-1-64971-832-7

CHAPTER ONE

Fred

The Dennisons had no idea what they were getting into when they let Josh have a party at the end of Exam Week, even though they were werewolves. As I straightened my arm to devour fourteen New York System wieners, I suspected they might understand now. The delivery guy from the hot dog joint had said his manager wouldn't send any more over. Mr. Dennison crossed them off a list and called a different place, ordering wings this time.

I headed to the tiki bar set up across from the empty food tables. I bumped Lane Meyer in the shoulder. He turned and hissed at me, then laughed when I fake-screamed at his fangs. Then, I dropped my glamour and showed him whose scary mouth was the boss.

"That never gets old for you, huh?" Lane tossed his long hair, blue this week, chuckling.

"Nope. You?" I scanned the bar for something to drink.

"Maybe in a century." Lane pulled the celery out of his Bloody Mary and tossed it at the trash. He missed. No one cared.

"Where's the kegs?"

"You must have drunk them all, man."

"Oh. Well, dang it." I snapped my fingers.

"You sound like your old man when you say 'dang it,' dude." Lane raised an eyebrow.

"And you sound like a surfer when you say dude, bro." I snorted.

"I am a surfer. Sort of. And now you sound like a meathead, mofo." Lane put one hand on his hip.

"They say you are what you eat, so I am a meathead. Sort of." I grinned, then winked. "And now you sound like a hipster."

"Harsh!" Lane winced. "Ow, sick burn!"

"Coulda been worse. I could be a Spectral Magus."

"Thank the gods of rock-and-roll you're not." Lane smiled. "Last thing I need is a literal ray of sunshine."

We laughed harder than one of Lane's concerts rocked. My fanged buddy fell off his barstool, Bloody Mary and all. But he didn't spill a single drop.

"Epic vampire reflexes, Lane."

"That's what she said, Fred."

"Eww, d-bag central." A vaguely familiar girl with straight dark hair down her back brushed past me to grab a fifth of vodka off the bar. She tumbled some into the red plastic cup in her hand, then poured cherry cola on top. I couldn't read the Sharpie-inscribed name on it, just the letter "I." She stalked away, huffier than a steam engine. I stared.

"Where's your snappy comebacks now, Fred?" Lane held up his drink with one hand and brushed himself off with the other.

"Huh?" I scratched behind my ear. Redcaps don't scratch our heads because of our caps. At least they don't itch.

"The last time a chick dissed us for being d-bags, you said something about tea bags."

"Oh. Forgot." I hadn't. I just didn't want to for some reason I couldn't define just then. But I couldn't admit that to Lane.

"Whatevs, mofo. It's totes cray-cray to hear you hold back like that at a party." Lane winked. "According to your hipster friend, at least."

"Dude, I'm this close to having to tithe." I put my thumb and forefinger together to demonstrate. "Cut me some slack. Be a hipster friend, not a hipster fiend."

"I'm gonna miss you, Fred." Lane leaned on the bar, staring into his drink instead of kicking it back. It was like an arrow to the heart for me sometimes, the way he could go from roll on the floor laughing to down in the dumps. His mood swings didn't seem to have that kind of effect on most other people, but that made sense, at least. He was one of my best friends, after all.

"It's only for a year." I slapped my hand on the tiki bar for emphasis. It only shook a little.

"And a day." Lane leaned his chin on one hand.

"Thanks for the reminder, I needed that." I elbowed him. "You'll be fine."

"Man, I don't know. I thought you'd actually avoid being on the five-year plan." Lane turned his head, looking up at me. "Ever since we were Academic Probation twins in Freshman year, I've been using you as an example to follow."

"At least it's faerie magic pulling me away and not bad grades." I shrugged. "The example will still be there, even when I'm not."

"Yeah, yeah." Lane's head shot up at the sound of guitar feedback. "Dang it, dude, That's my cue."

"Knock em undead, bro!" I waved at Lane as he stepped up on the patio Night Creatures had set up as a stage.

As the opening riffs to *The Sweater Song* by Weezer started, I walked around the back of the allegedly kegless bar. The steel in my work boot's toe bumped something that clanged. I should have known our pack's Umbral Magus did a spell to play "hide the keg from the Redcap." I felt around with my hands until I found the tap, then laid on my back to get my mouth under it. After that, I reached up and opened wide, about to pull the tap and deliver foamy, hoppy goodness to my taste-buds.

"Now, you hold it right there, Redford!" a playful female voice called. "Smile!"

"Huh?" What felt like a zillion camera flashes blinded me.

"Oh em gee, Instagram that now, Kim!" Only one man I knew actually talked in leet-speak. Well, maybe he was a dragon man. Well, maybe he was just a dragon.

"Oh, come on, Trogdor the Blaineanator." I reached for the tap, not caring whether I had spots in my eyes at that point. "Can't a guy get a drink at a bar for crying out loud?"

"Sure, a guy can. But a Redcap shouldn't drink the Special Reserve all by himself." Josh stepped out from behind Blaine and picked up the keg. I knew he had to be enhancing his strength with wolf shifter power to do it. "I had Maddie hide this so we all could have some. You get one pint, just like the rest of us. After that, find something else to drink." He handed me the red cup he'd just poured, and I downed it in one go.

"Sure, fine, okay, whatever." I sat up and spotted the dark-haired girl's leftover vodka. "This'll do."

With the bottle as my companion, I pushed through the crowd back toward the food table. Chicken wings had arrived. I looked up to see Beth, Josh's sister, staring right at me. She put a phone to her ear, propped her prosthetic leg up on a picnic table, and ordered thirty pu pu platters. Good call on her part. I gave her a mental thumbs up since my hands were full of honey sriracha wings. And screaming buffalo wings. And blue cheese dressing. And habanero bacon wings. Wings Over Providence was the best. I'd miss them more than beer once I went to the Under. I sighed.

"You need some wet-naps, Fred?" Jeannie La Montagne always seemed to know what was missing in any given situation, like the Mom friend she is. I nodded instead of answering, realizing she'd probably already caught on to the fact that I was more bitter than sweet about this party.

"It's not so bad, Fred." I took the moist towelettes from Jeannie and turned to see her djinn boyfriend, Ismail. "The king orders takeout, you know."

"Did they have takeout back in 1916 or whenever it was you tithed?" I tossed the dirty napkins at a trash can and made it this time. "Three points!"

"Two." Ismail shook his head. "And no, but Gemma Tolland told me the king let her grandfather bring in pizza during her year and a day. That was in 2013."

"Good to know," I grinned. "But you should grab some wings while you have the chance because I'm not slowing down the old gullet for that piece of gossip."

Jeannie and Ismail each grabbed a basket of wings, and I went back to polishing the rest off. It was definitely stress-eating, but I told myself I could keep going since wolfing down a truck-ton of food helped power my magic. We'd been getting randomly attacked by a heavy-hitting Extramagus since December, so I had an excuse to keep my strength up.

I dumped a whole basket of wings in my mouth, not much caring about the sauce dripping down my chin. Or the bones. Redcap digestion rocks. We can literally eat anything because that's how our faerie magic works. I chewed, thinking about how Public Enemy Number One's attacks had gone down up until this point. I had something wrong.

The attacks weren't random. That Extramagus had targeted members of Josh's pack with laser precision. Lynn Frampton almost died, so did Henry Baxter. Maddie May and Nox Phillips almost lost their magic. Josh got poisoned by a cockatrice, and when Kim Ichiro used a Luck charm to save him, her dad aged about twenty years. Blaine's step-dad did actually die. Professor Watkins was still technically breathing, but only because no one could find his brother to ask if they should pull the plug.

I was next. Everyone in the pack knew. Probably PPC's Headmistress Thurston, too, by now. But she was also in the hospital. It'd be especially bad for me if Ismail's theory were right and the Extramagus sided with the Sidhe Queen. My dad was one of the king's Dukes, and I loved him more than almost anyone in the world. The magical jerk always targeted two people who either loved each other already or were destined to. So, someone in my immediate family had to be the other target.

Mama almost never left the house, and she had a veritable army of ghosts protecting her everywhere she went. But my brother had to go to school for the rest of the week which was warded against anything without a body. That Extramagus wouldn't be heartless enough to attack a ten-year-old kid like Ed in the middle of a school day, would he?

"Hey Fred, usually you're the one devouring everything, but what's eating you?"

"Urp!" I turned around to see Tony Gitano at the edge of the shadows by a round stone table. When I beckoned to him, he just shook his head, crossed his arms, and jerked his chin at the table. I snagged the rest of the wings, headed his way, and held out a basket of wings to him.

"Thanks, but I'm not hungry." Tony nodded but kept his arms crossed. "Which is good because I'm not really on the guest list, anyway."

"They aren't either, but Josh isn't kicking them out." I pointed an elbow off toward a crowd of Magi and changelings who kept to a day schedule. "Come on, Tony. At least sit down while I eat and drink." I jerked my chin at the stone table.

"Fine." He sighed, glancing off toward where a certain platinum-haired owl shifter danced to The Night Creatures covering the best song ever, Golden Slumbers by The Beatles. "Just don't say I didn't warn you. I'm on the pack's naughty list. But it's your party. I won't make you drink alone."

"Thanks, man. I understand why you'd probably rather dance

than sit here with me. Grab that vodka?" I gestured with the baskets of wings covering my hands and most of my forearms.

"Sure thing." Tony snagged the bottle I'd left on the food table, which now looked like a wing night nightmare.

He took a swig, then winked before sitting at the stone patio table with me. The rest of Josh's Tinfoil Hat pack thought Tony was more than a little hinky, possibly suspicious. I didn't. We'd worked for Dad together since High School. I always thought Tony meant well, even when his methods and motives seemed muddy. He couldn't help it. His Mafioso dad didn't give him the best example growing up.

"You mind if I drop the glamour?" I looked around. No one else was over in that corner of the Dennison's ginormous yard.

"Go ahead. That'd be great." Tony proceeded not to flinch or even blink as the pointed ears, gray skin, and sharklike teeth of my actual appearance revealed itself. Actually, he grinned, which was nothing new for Tony. I always wondered why and figured it was about time I asked.

"How come all this never freaks you out?" I ate the paper baskets the wings came in. Why? They had bacon and delicious sauce all over them. Redcaps can digest paper and all kinds of stuff other people can't, with no problem. And apparently, cat shifters like Tony could watch like it was the most normal thing in the world. I ran my tongue out to lick my fingers, worried when I noticed the beginning of a fork in it.

"I've seen too much, man. You don't even know." He shrugged, then pushed the vodka in my direction. The bottle was still three-quarters full, so I guzzled it. Alcohol didn't do much to Redcaps, even as changelings. It'd take a case of fifths to get me tipsy on any other night. I had no idea nothing was normal just then.

"Fire in the belly!" I giggled, then blinked. Tony tilted up around the edges. No, he didn't. That was the edge of my vision.

"You better go to the Under, like tomorrow. You should have

done it yesterday." Tony sighed. "But even Gnomes can't go that far back in time."

"I know. But I couldn't. Can't." I took another pull from the bottle, then peered blearily at the label. Regular plain old vodka shouldn't make everything spinnier than a gyroscope. Whee!

"You have to, or you'll break some laws." Tony glanced over at the Night Creatures. Well, not really. He kept on looking at the girls dancing in front of them. No, just the same one from before —Olivia Adler, the owl shifter who took Ritalin so she could be diurnal. I didn't understand what Tony's deal was with her. Girls are just people, like guys. Before I asked, he went on, "Exams are over. What's stopping you from going already? I mean, what about tonight? Things could really suck for you if you stay any longer. You could go now."

"Got a job tomorrow morning." I blinked and shook my head, wondering why I wanted to sleep my bleariness off suddenly. "Should only take half the day. I can wait that long."

"You really should call in tithed to work, man," Tony grinned, creepier than the Cheshire cat. For once, that hinky smile unsettled me. My vodka-marinaded brain couldn't wrap around why.

"Can't. 'S for Misser Kazsschin—um—Kazymin—uh—Kazynski." I leaned my head on my hand and missed. The stone table felt icy, refreshing like the glass of water I probably should have had instead of grain alcohol. The carvings in the stone were lumpy but reminded me of those old fashioned rubber ice bags, the kind you dump cubes into and then use as a pillow. "He broke 'is hip. Gotta build 'im a ramp, make doors bigger. Hey, why can't I talk?"

"Slipped you a magical mickey, Fred." Tony reached out toward the cap on top of my head, then winced as I slapped it away. "Sorry, man, but this is how it's gotta be."

"Ugh." That lame slap had taken all my strength. "Need my cap. Jerk."

"I know. That's why I have to take it." He reached out again, and there wasn't a thing I could do to stop him. I could barely believe he'd touch the thing, especially without the glamour making it look like a Paw Sox hat. Without glamour, my cap was gnarly. Also sticky. Cats can't handle sticky stuff, so I kept telling myself Tony wouldn't really take it, right up until the moment he did.

A tingle of magic made the hair on my head stand on end. Even the stuff under my cap. Whatever device Tony was using to touch it had passive magic, but it was persistent. I wondered what kind of magipsychic gadget he had there, especially since the magic in it felt and smelled like faerie. There was no way for a cat shifter like Tony to have his own magic. Only four items like that existed. All of them were way too rich for Tony's blood, and three were for the wrong shifter species.

"There." I heard Tony moving away. The tingle stopped, and the stone table heated under my cheek, almost like the sun warmed it. "Now it's all set."

"All set what now?" But I was alone. Tony had gone. So had my senses.

"Fred!" A big hand clapped me on the shoulder, and the voice that came with it had a Cajun accent. My friend Bobby Tremain, the bear shifter, had an accent like that. "Fred! You gotta get up, big guy, come on."

"Come on, Big Red." I felt another hand on my other side, lifting my arm. "Well, maybe that's not a good thing to say, under the circumstances." I wondered what circumstances Blaine Harcourt meant, exactly.

"Can it, Trogdor. And both of you get out of my way." The snarky woman could only be Lynn, Bobby's mate. "This is serious business." Fingers that felt more like icicles pressed against my neck, and I shivered. "Pulse is normal all things considered. Sit him up, then open his mouth."

"You have any idea how risky that is with his glamour dropped like that?" That was Blaine again with his typical dragonish paranoia.

"Yeah, and I don't care. A passed out Redcap is way less dangerous than a rampaging one."

I wondered which Redcap they meant. I was drunk with a full stomach. No way I'd rampage. At least not unless the worst thing in the world had happened. Everything from after I had found the chicken wings was hazy. But I remembered Tony doing something distinctly un-Tony-like. I tried to touch my head, but moving my arm felt like moving a mountain.

"My cap?" I opened my eyes to find Lynn shining a flashlight into my mouth while Blaine peered over her shoulder, his eyes red with vertical slits like a reptile. That meant he was checking my magic energy. Made sense.

"It speaks." Blaine gazed at the top of my head. "This is beyond weird. But enough about me. What do you see, Doctor Frampton?"

"Everything's normal. And it shouldn't be under these circumstances. Totally weird, unless it just happened." She turned the light off and moved aside. "And I'm not a doctor. Yet."

"It's all weird, how?" I tried to thank Bobby for asking the question my mouth couldn't form.

"All his vitals match the ones I took during the zillion hours of practice Fred helped me with back during mid-terms." Lynn's cold fingers prodded my wrist this time. "This is medically inconclusive. He should have elevated everything right now. Is there any chance his cap's not really gone?"

"Yeah, I can't really answer that, so it's also magically inconclusive." Blaine grabbed me by the shoulders and pointed at the top of my head. "I only see the world's worst case of hat hair with normal eyes, but a truck-ton of faerie magic with dragon eyes.

The weird part is no cap with regular sight since Fred always glamours on a Paw Sox hat. There's magic around his head. Without his cap, there shouldn't be any magic there, at least according to every textbook I've read on the subject. The absence of hat should make a vortex, sucking magic from everyone and everything else around. But it's like someone put a stopper in it that I can't see with either sight. The only way that's possible is if someone glamoured his head. But why anyone would do that is beyond me."

"Could it be some kind of practical joke, maybe?" Bobby peered down at me, scratching his head. "Hey, maybe he got drunk and made it invisible, put one over on us. Is that what you did, Fred?"

I tried to tell Bobby I'd never make my cap invisible, but only an incoherent gurgle came out of my mouth. I wasn't sure whether my garbled speech came from being drunk or having a mouthful of Redcap teeth hanging out. Probably a bit of both. I hoped Bobby was right about someone playing a prank. Because I couldn't remember about Tony and what had actually happened at that point.

"I'm not sure he's in a state to answer you." I smiled when I saw Henry Baxter. The bookish Psychic vampire had more common sense than most of my friends. He'd know what to do. "We ought to get him home so—" He leaned on the table, reaching out with the other hand as though about to help me. "Oh." Henry froze, his eyes going even more out of focus than I imagined my own had.

"Great. A trip down memory lane." Lynn sat down across from me. What felt like ten minutes and ten seconds all at the same time passed as they waited for Henry to snap out of his Psychic trance.

"Yeah, we should get Fred home." Henry took his hand off the table and wiped it against his leg, as though trying to get rid of something icky. "His family will know what to do for him."

"Aren't you going to tell us what you saw?" Blaine tapped his foot. "It looked important."

"Nope." Henry shrugged. "Important or not, it involves a secret I agreed to keep. As a matter of fact, I ought to go wipe out that memory. It's dangerous, but I can't tell anyone why. Probably should stop thinking about it, too. You never know who's a Telepath."

"Well, that's amazeballs dipped in awesome sauce." Lynn rolled her eyes so much it made me dizzy. "Super memory power, and we can't even use the info he gets from it."

Bobby and Blaine bookended me, getting their shoulders under my arms to stand me up. My stomach decided to act like a Maytag on the spin cycle. Something splattered on the tile and stank to high heaven.

"Woah!" Henry's vampire reflexes helped him jump back just in time, taking Lynn with him. I managed to make it without upchucking again.

I wasn't sure exactly how they got me to the driveway or how long it took before Josh pulled up in his dad's Campus Security cruiser, but I remembered nothing else after they bundled me into the back. The way I felt the next morning, that was a good thing.

CHAPTER TWO

Irina

I'd been up since before five in the morning, clearing knick-
knacks and trinkets out of Grandpa's bathroom and living room,
plus the hallways leading to it and the bedroom. I'd decided no
one could possibly have more trinkets and souvenirs than Saul
Kazynski. Crashing that crazy PPC party the night before hadn't
taken the edge off visiting the city I hated. But I loved my
Grandpa. This was the third time I'd returned because he
needed me.

Every time I visited my once and hopefully not future home,
something craptastic happened. It's why I never came back on
holiday breaks from the Boston Conservatory. Instead, I volun-
teered to water people's plants, walk their dogs, clean up after
their cats, and still pay loads of sublet rent money in Boston all
winter and summer. Now, I had my own apartment with the
most normal regular human roommate in the known universe
since Junior year. And I'd graduated the night before that concert
at the senior center benefit, so I thought it'd be safe enough. But
I'd been wrong.

And that concert was craptastic crap on a crap cracker, too. I didn't care that all the extrahumans had called the thing in Water Place Park a golem. It looked like something straight outta Lovecraft. I hate Lovecraft. He hated everything so much all his stories are about destroying the world. He should have changed his name to Hatecraft.

Even that horror writer up in Maine might have freaked out faced with that golem. And, of course, Irina Kazynski was expected by her faerie monarch honored Grandpa just to keep on playing through all the insanity. Our music helped defend people, at least, which is how it's supposed to go for Psychic musicians like me. But I was rusty in the non-human powers department. I hadn't been fast enough, and Grandpa's hip got busted.

So, there I was, waiting for the magical construction guy from Redford Renovations to arrive and get to work modifying the place for wheelchair and walker access. Grandpa had a broken hip. The folks down at the Physical Therapy and Rehabilitation Center said he'd be fine to go to a home, but not on his own, or without accommodations. Apparently, this apartment needed as much rehabilitation as his broken hip.

I wiped my forehead with a cloth, realized it was the one I'd been dusting with, then screamed in frustration. I didn't worry about people hearing me. The second floor was vacant, and the guy on the third floor was in jail for some kind of crime against extrahumanity. Still, the neighborhood hadn't gone downhill, just Grandpa's building. Bad for him since most of his income came from rent. He'd stopped taking new violin students six months ago.

In the kitchen, I splashed cold water on my face and dumped the dirty dust rag in a bucket. With a fresh one tucked in my back pocket, I went back to the living room to tie my hair back again in the mirror. I worried about having to stay here even longer to clear out Brodsky's apartment and help screen new tenants for two units. After all, I'd gone to school for music, not landladying. I screamed again, this time with extra blood-curdle. It made me feel a little better. At least, at first it did.

"Um, I wasn't interrupting anything, I hope?" The rich baritone voice startled me. I whirled, almost knocking over a spindly aluminum music stand. A hammy hand righted it before I could move. It belonged to a big guy with a bird's nest of unkempt hair, making me think he usually wore a hat. I recognized him immediately.

"You're the lunk from last night." I put my hands on my hips.

"Hey, you're the vodka lady." He flashed me a smile I didn't return, despite his perfect-looking teeth. I knew he was an Extrahuman. The teeth could be fake or glamoured. At least his expression wasn't coy or flirty. I wouldn't have tolerated a hungover contractor trying to put the moves on me, regular human or not.

"It's Irina. Miss Kazynski, to you." I narrowed my eyes, peering up into his pallid face. Something seemed off about him besides the aftereffects of too much drinking. "Are you sure you can handle working today?"

"Sure thing, Miss Kazynski." He reached up as though about to tip his cap to me, but his head was bare.

"Look, maybe you should have called in sick or something." I walked over to the big bay window at the front of the parlor, reaching for my phone. "You're looking more than a little green around the gills."

"Sorry, but you're stuck with me." He shook his head, then touched his temple and winced. "Already tried that. Anyway, this is my last job. After this, I'll get some rest. Dad said, no excuses."

He pulled a tape measure off his belt and went around the room. It had to be a magipsychic device because the measure inched its way up doorframes and down walls. The lunk jotted numbers down on a card. I peered at them, trying to make sense of how the writing could look so tidy when his hands dwarfed the pencil stub.

"Excuses?" I raised an eyebrow, then got angry because that kind of thing causes premature wrinkles. Electric violin-playing YouTube stars had to stay cute, not end up with a face like DeForest Kelley. "Oh, wait a minute. I bet you told him you didn't drink that much."

"Well, that's because I didn't." He sighed. It sounded wistful as though maybe he'd drank like a sailor on shore leave to impress a girl or something. What had he meant by this being his last job? How could a garden-variety hangover make anyone so fatalistic? He didn't sound nearly as dude-bro lunkish as he had the night before.

"Your dad's one thing, but does your boss know you came to work half in the bag?" I noticed the sound of something tapping before realizing it was my foot. My left hand had curled as though it held my fiddle. If I started playing with a Psychic boost, I could send him packing in under a minute. I crossed the room, on my way to grab it, but the quality of the contractor's silence stopped me in my tracks.

"Now you just wait one minute, Miss Irina Kazynski, star of the Internet screen." The lunk's jaw clenched, getting squarer than 4/4 time. "Hungover isn't drunk. Someone I thought I could trust spiked my drink. Oh, and by the way, my dad is my boss. He's in the Under on important business for the Goblin King, too. If I don't do this job, it's not getting done. You wanna try calling him? Be my guest." His scowl relaxed into a wistful half-grin. Somehow, I knew missing his dad had him more upset than my snobbish behavior.

Instead of gasping, I inhaled slowly. Instead of stale beer, he smelled of cedar and sawdust. I blinked. I waited for the other shoe to drop, for him to get upset that I hadn't apologized and lose his temper. This guy was either a Magus or Fae, and every one of either group I'd met had short fuses. Things in Providence always went sideways for me, sliding into craptastic no matter what I did to make things better. But if I pissed this guy off enough, it'd be my own damn fault for once. And I couldn't abide that. I also wasn't sure I could apologize even if I should. I hadn't felt so immature since my Sophomore year in High School.

"Well, I guess it's my fault for forgetting my manners." He pocketed the pencil stub and card. "I should have introduced myself like Mama taught me." He grinned and held out his right hand. "I'm Fred Redford."

"Oh." I stared at his huge hand, then looked at my much smaller one. It'd get crushed if he had anything like a firm hand-shake. I closed my eyes and wondered what Grandpa would do. Shake it, of course. I'd expected the calluses, but his were thicker than mine. "Well, hello, then."

"So, is it cool if I keep on working here?" He crooked a finger at the still inching tape measure, and it headed toward him.

"Yeah, it's cool. Go on and do your job." I grabbed my violin and its case and headed toward the kitchen. I stopped, glancing over my shoulder to find him opening a red metal toolbox. "You want some soda or something? Grandpa always has ginger ale."

"Wow, thanks." His smile was definitely way too perfect. He just had to be using some kind of glamour. "In a bit. I have to give the tools their instructions and get some special plaster from the truck." He headed out the door.

In the kitchen, I rummaged in the fridge for something to drink. I couldn't do ginger ale unless I wanted to burp while practicing. I didn't. A pitcher of iced tea squatted in the back, so I reached for that and poured a glass, relieved to have a cold bever-age. Summer was coming on early and with a vengeance.

I hoped Fred Redford wasn't the type to let the ambient temperature get to him. If he was Fae and Unseelie that might be the case. Maybe my guess about him being a Magus had been wishful thinking. I minded them the least of all the extrahumans. I tried to tell myself the son couldn't have taken after the father. Most his age were already in the Under, tithing to one of the monarchs. Everyone knew Neil Redford was a Redcap. His glamour-free face freaked people out all along I-95 from Pawtucket to Cranston on billboards. But I hadn't heard much about Fred or the Mama he'd mentioned.

I dried my hands, then moved my violin next to Grandpa's. I lifted the lid, sighing as I admired the amber-stained wood, the scroll, the chin-rest. That violin, like Grandpa himself, had seen things I wouldn't wish into the nightmares of my enemies. I shivered, a sudden chill coming over me as my eye snagged on the two seals embossed in the velvet interior of the case.

The queen and the king had both given their favor to Saul Kazynski over half a century ago, and it'd pass to me along with the violin eventually whether I liked it or not. I didn't. The Stradivarius would end up locked in an attic somewhere while I sawed out Internet hits on my Stingray if it meant I could avoid anything Extrahuman for the rest of my life.

"Hey." Fred stood in the doorway, hands framing the biggest lunchbox I'd ever seen. "Just letting you know that the tools are widening the doorways now that they have plaster and glue." He glanced around at the boxes and bags of stuff I'd moved to the kitchen. "I'll go have my lunch on the stoop." He turned his back on the kitchen. I imagined someone stabbing him in it, probably because he'd mentioned his friend spiking his drink. I got a bad hunch about him going outside, something I usually ignored in Boston. But I couldn't afford that luxury in Providence.

"No, wait." I dropped the lid to cover the Stradivarius and shuffled things around. "Use the table. I already ate." I pulled a chair out, scraping it on the linoleum floor to be sure he'd hear, then invoked the name any faerie from Providence wouldn't ignore. "Grandpa Kazynski would insist."

"Hmm." Fred looked me over. It wasn't anything like someone checking me out, more like he wanted to make sure I was okay with being around him. His gaze held admiration and respect, nothing sexual at all, which was fine by me. I've got no time for that. Fred was just about the strangest man I'd ever met. Almost as odd as me. "Okay. If you say so."

"You go to that Paranormal College, right?"

"Yeah. Extrahuman Engineering." He raised an eyebrow as though waiting for me to say he didn't look like the type for such a brainy subject. "And you don't."

"Nope."

"That's interesting." He sounded like he actually thought it was. "I saw you at Water Place Park, Jeannie's charity thing. You played while everyone else fought. Did you get your Psychic training somewhere else?" I couldn't help but stare as he brought fifteen sandwiches out of his lunchbox, arraying them on the table like an all-you-can-eat sandwich buffet.

"Well, I picked regular plain old human music to major in." I waved a hand at the violin cases. "Which is why I want to ask you something. But only if you promise not to tell anyone I'm an ignorant weirdo."

"Your weirdness is safe with me." I wasn't sure how he could talk around what for me would be seven mouthfuls of that meatball sub, but he managed.

The fact of the matter was, most Extrahumans had left Boston after the Internment. Once I went home, I might not find anyone to ask. And Fred seemed awfully good-natured for a guy with a hangover, changeling or not. I took a deep breath and a chance.

"Did you ever hear of someone being jinxed?" I couldn't look at him, but not because he was chewing monster bites of sandwich. More like I didn't think I could look at anyone after asking something like that. "And I'm not talking about that weird Luck stuff the raccoon-dog people deal with, either. I mean like a hex. Well, I know those don't really exist, but there has to be something like a curse or a—well, there's just no better word I can think of. A jinx. You know, just a 'bad things will happen to this person if they go to this place' kind of thing."

"Huh." Fred cleared his throat and actually put his sandwich down. I counted the remains of his lunch to avoid looking at him, realizing it had been the tenth. "Well, yeah, maybe. I guess coincidence could work like the old definition of a jinx." He tossed the rest of that tenth sandwich into his mouth, then picked up the eleventh. Half of it disappeared in seconds. I watched him finish it, carefully gaging whether he'd try to flirt if I gave him the idea I was some kind of lame damsel in distress. But I wasn't one, and he had another think coming if he decided I was.

"Well, I think I am." I hid my face behind the huge glass of iced tea I'd left sweating on the counter. "Jinxed, that is."

"It's scary, isn't it?" Fred stared at the stub of sandwich number twelve, then popped in his mouth.

"Excuse me?" I blinked. "Do you actually believe me about all this, or are you just humoring me because you have to work here all day?"

"Oh, I believe you, all right. I should have said I think it's pretty scary myself. Coincidence coming to call, I mean. My Magus friends say it can stick you in a bad pattern and screw you over. I know it's coming—" His teeth closed around the thirteenth sandwich, and he wrinkled his nose. "Ugh. Mama always uses such a heavy hand with the pesto." He dropped the sandwich and covered his neck with his hands. His skin went past pale and straight to gray. I'd waited too many tables in Freshman year not to know what that meant. Fred was choking. He couldn't breathe.

I didn't realize I'd dropped my glass until I heard it shatter. I didn't care. My arms barely reached around him, but it had to be enough. Pulling up and back with as much force as I could manage had done the trick the last time someone choked on my watch, figuratively, of course. This time, not so much.

I had strong arms from holding up a violin and bow for hours at a time, but Fred Redford was a huge guy, bigger than he appeared, like something in a rear-view mirror. It was a question of strength for me, not leverage. I let go and stepped to his side instead. Then, I used every bit of force I could and slammed his chest against the corner of Grandpa's kitchen table. His phone clattered to the floor. Good thing he used an Otterbox case.

A chunk of barely chewed bread, meat, and basil paste flew in an arc, then spattered against the wall. Fred hacked a ragged cough, then started breathing again. I coughed, too. That's a lie. I sank to my knees on the floor, sobbing. Fred hunkered down on the floor, kneeling across from me as he picked up the glass and dumped it in the trash bin.

"I'm sorry." I watched him, stomach in knots as I waited to see if he'd cut half his hand off.

"Why?"

"Because you choking, the glass, it's all my fault. Every time I come to Providence, bad things happen. It's the jinx or the coincidence or whatever you want to call it."

"Hmm." Fred stood up, grabbing a paper towel to clean up the lump of food that had almost killed him. He even got a bottle of Lysol to spray the spot and wipe it. "No."

"Wait, no?" I blinked. "What do you mean?" I couldn't take no for an answer, not on this. "Disaster strikes every time I come back, ever since I left. And this is the third time I've been back this year. It's going to be terrible when it finally happens, whatever it is."

"Well, you can rest easy." Fred tossed the paper towels in the trash, covering the glass. "It's not you, it's me. I pissed off an Extramagus." He sighed. "They manipulate coincidence. And I have to leave for the Under as soon as I'm done with this job. It means he'll go after my family instead."

"Oh, Fred." I put my hands on my cheeks. He was wrong. This was all my fault, no matter what he said. "No. I'm so sorry. It's not you, it's me. This is way older than you pissing off a powerful weirdo. You see, it all goes back to Grandpa's—"

His phone rang. I picked it up, answered it, and put it on speaker. The voice at the other end proved me right, or so I thought.

CHAPTER THREE

Fred

"Freddie, is Ed with you?" Mama's voice dropped an octave in pitch when she was nervous. Her Cranston accent still had the same nasal vowels, though.

"No, Mama." I took a deep breath, trying to tell myself it was nothing. "Remember, I'm at Mr. Kazynski's for the job."

"I know, sonny boy, but sometimes he follows you to watch the tools." Mama sounded worse than my stomach felt. "He's hidden to watch without you knowing before. I'd feel better if you'd at least look for him, *capisce?*"

"Okay, Mama. I'll check around the building." I hadn't smelled Ed, though. Then again, nothing even remotely connected to my digestive system seemed to work right that morning, so I strode across the kitchen and peered out the window. No sign of my kid brother. "Mama, I'm going to go outside and walk around." I looked at the young woman who'd just saved my life. I thought I could trust her to hold the phone for a few minutes after something like that. "This is Irina, Mr. Kazynski's granddaughter. She'll be right here on the line with you." I gazed into Irina's blue eyes and watched them close as she nodded. "If Ed comes in while I'm out there, she'll let you know. Just hang on, and I'll be right back."

I walked three times around the building, counterclockwise like any future self-respecting vassal of the Goblin King would. No sign of Ed. I headed across the street and peered up at windows in on the second floor and in the adjacent buildings. Nothing. I even screwed the ghost-detecting monocle Mama had made for me into one eye and looked around for my brother's deceased friend Bob or any other dead people. No one. I made it back to the Kazynskis' building before those twelve sandwiches danced in the pit of my stomach like a dozen enchanted princesses without fancy dresses.

For the second time in twenty-four hours, I hurled. And this time, none of my friends were there to help me recover. Redcaps puking is serious business, and not just because we can eat more than an elephant. Our brand of special includes being able to eat literally anything, and keep it down, too. Mama's sandwiches, despite her heavy hand with the pesto, had never come back up before. I leaned against the yellow vinyl siding, wondering what could possibly be wrong with me.

"You okay?" Bobby Tremain stood in the driveway, holding out a red and blue bandanna.

"No." I took the bandanna and mopped my forehead with it. I respected Bobby too much to use it on my mouth and risk shredding it. It was nearly impossible to glamour my teeth after vomiting. That's like a cat being unable to sheath its claws.

"Anything I can do?" The bear shifter hunkered down to peer at me, concern creasing his forehead.

"I don't know. Because I'm not sure what's wrong with me." I shook my head. "Haven't felt right since last night, even though I barely remember it."

"Understood." Bobby nodded. "Can I get anyone for you?"

"My brother." I grimaced as my stomach churned again. "He's missing."

"No way." Bobby stood up straight, squaring his shoulders. He was just about the only other guy at PPC who came close to being my size. "I'll call Josh, get the whole pack out looking for him."

"Don't." Irina's voice came from the open kitchen window. "Your mom hung up, Fred. Something else happened."

"What, exactly?" Through the screen, I saw her jaw drop as she blinked up at the sky.

"Duck, Fred!" Bobby tackled me, fortunately away from the puddle of sick I'd made. It had already foamed up, degrading the asphalt. Redcaps have serious acid indigestion.

A whir like one of those drones people kept using to take pictures of WaterFire sounded next to my left ear. Bobby winced, and I smelled blood. Something crunched behind me. I propped myself up on my freshly skinned elbows and turned my head.

A paper airplane fluttered nearby, glowing as though a minia-ture sun were behind it. It wasn't since the crazy magical faerie paper had landed in the shade. All the sunshine meant was that someone infused it with Spectral magic before sending it. I reached out, but Bobby slapped my hand away.

"No, let him pick it up." Irina rested her forehead against the screen. "It's exactly like what Mrs. Redford said happened to her."

"Well, what is it?" Bobby cocked his head, making the face I'd come to think of as his "bearwildered" expression.

"A message." Irina leaned against the window frame.

"About what?" I ground my teeth together, nostrils flaring. But I didn't want to get angry at Irina, especially not after our uneasy truce back when I started the renovations plus the life-saving not-quite-Heimlich maneuver earlier.

"I don't know." Irina shrugged. "She hung up before opening it, but she mentioned grabbing it quick before anyone else touched it and got hurt."

"Well, but Fred's mom is a Psychic." Bobby shook his head and blinked as though something hurt. "He's a changeling planning on tithing Unseelie, and that thing smells like the queen's people. It might not be safe for him. I'll do it."

"No!" The word left my lips and Irina's at the same time. I glanced at her, wondering how much she knew, then continued. "It cut your ear."

"Huh." Bobby reached up and rubbed, wincing as fresh blood stained his fingers. "Weird. I'm a shifter. That should have healed over by now."

"Nope." I shook my head. "Magical wound. It won't heal until I read this. That's the queen's way of making sure she's never ignored. Weird delivery method aside, it's addressed to me, see?" I reached out and grabbed the paper projectile. It took most of my willpower not to just crumple the thing and toss it in the dumpster out back, but I had to open it. I didn't want Bobby Tremain walking around bleeding all day.

The flowing glowing script, like some kind of back-lit screen display only in fancy calligraphic writing, met my eyes. I scanned it, feeling my stomach twist into knots again. After that, I wanted to drop the rest of my glamour and roar at the top of my lungs, but a gaggle of Elementary school kids swarmed off a school bus at the end of the driveway.

I clenched my teeth instead, thinking of Ed, how he'd had nightmares for a month straight after seeing me like that when he was three. And I swore I wouldn't be the monster in a kid's head again if I could avoid it. But keeping up appearances had me feeling like I'd just swallowed molten lead. I toppled over on my side, trying not to lose my cookies again.

"Woah, Fred," Bobby's eyes went silvery as his bear responded to my obvious distress. "I'm calling 911." He reached for the phone in his pocket, but stopped, gazing up at the window.

Music poured out of the screen's gray mesh, smooth as silk and soothing as honey. Irina's head sat propped on the violin's chin-rest, her left hand curled around her instrument's neck. A horsehair bow extended from the fingertips of her right hand as though she'd been born holding it. The dry-heaves threatening my stomach, magic, and possibly my life, eased. I held up the letter, the wording more like plain ink now, though a hint of Spectral sparkle remained. My sweat- and tear-soaked face relaxed when I realized it'd be safe to unclench my jaw. I sat back, letting the now mundane paper drop into my lap.

"To the Redcap changeling known as Frederick Redford, I give you salutation. You have until the Under Clock strikes Thirteen to collect your brother from the castle at the center of my demesne, or he belongs to me forever," Bobby read. "But what's this funky symbol? Some kind of signature?"

"That's the mark of the Seelie Queen." I shook my head, then turned to look back in the kitchen window again. "I'm sorry, Irina. But I won't be able to finish your grandpa's renovations. I have to go to the Under right away."

She had her back to the window now though she still played. Her shoulders shook, but her music still sounded like magic. I headed back through the door to the building, then the one leading into the apartment. Bobby followed.

I snapped my fingers, then whistled to call off my enchanted tools. They rose in the air and dropped into their big red box. I went ahead and shut that with my hands, trying to conserve as much of my magic was left to go and get Ed. Even if my stomach had been fine, I had no idea whether there'd be anything safe to eat in the Seelie side of the Under. Seelie Redcaps hadn't been a thing since his Wild West days, according to Dad.

"Let me help you with that." Bobby held out his hand. "You don't want to waste any time. I'll get those tools back to your house."

"Bring the whole truck." I knew he could drive, so I tossed my keys at him. "Thanks, Bobby. I'm so lucky you showed up." I held the big red toolbox out, and he took it.

"You should thank Tony." Bobby hefted the box. I was surprised he could carry it even though he was a big strong bear shifter. The metal was all faerie friendly, no iron. That plus the enchantments made them heavier than regular tools. "He called and told me to come check on you over here."

"Look, man. Tony spiked my drink last night, which is why you and Blaine had to carry me off the Dennison's property. I'm not sure I should thank that damn cat for anything."

"You decide who to trust." Bobby shrugged, almost losing his grip. "I believe in him enough for both of us. Anyway, you do what you gotta. I'll call Josh, tell him what's going on."

"What about your dad, Fred?" Irina stood in the kitchen doorway, the light behind her, making it hard to see the expression on her face. "He's a duke, right? Can't he go and help you out?"

"No." I sighed. "The letter was addressed to me specifically. Unless Dad was invited, him setting foot in the queen's part of the Under would be an act of war. He can't do it. Ismail and Nox can't help, either. Unseelie djinn and Kelpies are under the same restriction. I'm untithed, so it's up to me to get Ed back."

"But you need help. You can't do something like that alone." Bobby shook his head. "Can't you bring Blaine? He's powerful when he's not freaking out, and his mom's a friend of the queen's. She couldn't possibly object to him being in the Under."

"Oh, she can if he comes with me." I swallowed past a lump in my throat. "I'm the named party in the letter, and this whole situation smacks of a Quest. Blaine's got way more magic than me. Anyone helping has to be lower on the Extrahuman totem pole than I am. All the magic shifters are a step up from changelings. And that's why I can't bring Ren Ichiro, even though Selkies like him are Seelie and allowed in the queen's lands."

"Well, then. We leave the truck here. I'll go." Bobby's nostrils flared. I shook my head, all set to explain why regular shifters didn't fare well in the Under. Irina beat me to the punch.

"I already heard that you're a bear shifter. Your name's Bobby, right?" Irina hadn't moved from the door. Her voice sounded tired, resigned, nearly hopeless.

"Yeah. Bobby Tremain." He shrugged and glanced down at his full hands to indicate that he'd have offered a handshake if he could have.

"Look, it's awesome that you want to help your boy Fred, but you'll be stuck as a bear." Irina put her violin and bow away. "I might not know the fine points about invitations, but everyone's their truest Extrahuman self in the Under, which means all animals all the time for you shifters. There are ways around it with amulets, but they cost a fortune. Anyway, you don't have to worry. I'm going with Fred. It's the least I can do after jinxing him." The silhouette of her head tilted in my direction. "In case you haven't noticed, I'm Psychic."

Bobby stood there, opening and closing his mouth like a baby bird. I waited, watching him decide to leave the dramatic rescues to someone else for a change. He blinked, set his jaw, then nodded. After that, he said goodbye and left. I waited until the truck started and headed down the street before speaking.

"Irina, your grandpa's in the hospital. You're the only family he has. It's dangerous in the Under, especially for someone without any magic. Don't risk yourself for me." I stepped toward the kitchen, hoping she'd move aside and let me collect the last of my sandwiches. She didn't.

"I'm not doing it for you. Fred, your brother's in the queen's castle. You're the only one she named to get him back. You have to bring someone with less magic than you who can play nice with Seelies, and none of your friends fit the bill. That leaves me. I won't bother telling you not to risk yourself, but it's dangerous to go alone. Don't." She put her hands on her hips. I could see her face clearly now: the sadness in blue eyes with damp corners, the flat line of her mouth. "Besides, what are you going to do if you vomit again? They don't have Pepto Bismol in the Under. You already know I can help with that."

"But why?"

"It's a long story. If I tell it, we'll never make it in time." I had the idea Irina was glossing over the facts, but maybe she'd talk about it later. Her hand hovered over the box containing her own instrument. Then she shook her head. She latched her grandpa's violin case and hefted it. "I have a few other things to grab before we leave. Should change clothes, too. I'll only be a minute."

"Okay, same here. I'll have to go back to campus to get my bag of tricks, though."

"That's fine. There's an Under Gate over there, too." Irina headed out of the kitchen and through the living room. How did she know where the Gates were?

I waited while she got ready, wondering what in the name of the Goblin King could possess someone like Irina, who seemed wary about Extrahuman anything, to help me in such a big way. It certainly wasn't because I'd shown up to a job hungover and puked outside her window. But she'd returned to a city she thought jinxed her to help her grandfather raise money for the Senior Center, then came back again after he got injured. Maybe she had a charitable heart under that high-strung professional musician veneer.

I shrugged off the woolen thoughts my mind had gathered and tried to clear my head. My brain went ahead and collected more. The Extramagus targeting me liked working with the Seelie side of faerie. Had I been right in thinking he'd pick both his victims from my family as Ed being held prisoner seemed to indicate or was Irina the other target? If so, what in the world had she done to piss him off?

Could Irina's fear of jinxes have something to do with the Extramagus? Blaine and his mate Kimiko might have been able to do some research and figure it out, but that wasn't my forte. I wasn't a mental powerhouse with anything but geometry. I picked up my phone, which was still on the kitchen floor, and sent them as much information as I could in a text message. Even if I didn't succeed, at least they'd have a chance at second-guessing the still largely unknown foe we'd been dealing with.

I leaned against the kitchen doorframe, holding my lunch box. I'd just have to jump into this quest with both feet and worry about the whys in whatever future coincidence had in store for me.

CHAPTER FOUR

Irina

The Nocturnal Lounge over at PPC was one of the strangest places I'd seen at that point in my life. It wasn't the jam-packed bookshelves or the mismatched vintage and antique furniture, but the way half of it floated in the air while one of those robot vacuum cleaners puttered around the top floor. I hadn't imagined there'd actually be ghosts moving things around in there, or a Psychic Medium who looked like she time-traveled to shop in 1965 conducting them. A scarred cherrywood buffet that served as a coffee counter wobbled, then slid diagonally out of the nook it occupied on its own. Well, not really. A ghost I couldn't see had to be moving it.

"Thanks, Horace," said the medium. She squeezed her way into a claustrophobic looking space between the wall and the counter. "Take it away, Miss Williams!"

A vacuum cleaner whooshed to life, letting the medium clean an otherwise-impossible-to-reach spot. I shook my head. Why did my own Psychic ability have to be so relatively useless? I'd have had Grandpa's front room done in under an hour instead of three with ghostly help. If I'd been a Medium instead of an Empath, maybe my family would have been spared back when I was a kid. The vacuum switched off, so I figured I'd follow its example and flip off my whole sucking vortex of tragic thoughts.

"Oh, hi, Fred!" The medium squirmed out of the tiny space and dropped the vacuum wand to wave. "Didn't expect anyone at this time of day."

"Yeah, I know. It's not even noon." Fred shrugged. "I have to get in the lockers." His lips twisted in contemplation as he studied a pile of what looked like portable stage sections blocking an alcove at the foot of the stairs.

"Okey-doke." The medium nodded at a spot off to my right. "You there, um, new guy?" She tilted her head, then smiled. "Colin, is it? Thanks for telling me. Could you move the stage so Fred can get his stuff, please?" A big study table set itself down in front of a built-in bookcase.

I felt a chilly stir of air and crossed my arms, gripping them through the billowy cotton fabric of my elbow-length sleeves as my teeth chattered. Maybe it wasn't so bad being an Empath instead of a Medium. I hated getting cold so much that I wore jeans and boots in summer. I also hated imagining a ghost sinking through the floor right next to me.

"Oh, jeez, my manners suck." Fred literally smacked his head. "Irina, this is Bianca. Bianca, Irina." He headed down the stairs.

"Hey, maybe she could help?" I pitched my voice to a whisper, taking advantage of the fact that my mouth was at Fred's ear level on the stairs.

"Help with what?" Bianca peered at me, then Fred. "Sorry to pry, but Miss Williams is a busybody, and I was just communing with her. She listened in on you guys even though I tell her not to all the time."

"Heh," Fred grinned. "Yeah, it's all good. I don't think Bianca will be much help, though. Ghosts from out here can't get into the Under. And the reverse is also true, mostly."

"Really?" I raised an eyebrow.

"Yeah." Bianca twirled the end of her braid, which was dyed a shade of cotton-candy pink. "The only ghosts over there are from people who died in the Under. Since most of those are tithed, their pledges keep them anchored to their monarch. The only way for them to move on is if their unfinished business can get done in the Under or the monarch lets them leave. But with the power struggle between them, neither lets ghosts come and go."

"Oh. I should have remembered that." Unlike Fred, I didn't smack my head. It made sense now why Mrs. Redford said it was hopeless and hung up the phone. She was one of the best Mediums in the whole state, but if she couldn't bring her dead friends, she wouldn't be much use on a rescue mission in the Under.

"Wait." Bianca blinked, squinting in my direction. She peered at me for a moment until the light of recognition, which meant she realized who I was, took over her face. "You're bringing Irina Kazynski to the Under?"

"Hey!" I couldn't help but stomp my foot. "I'm standing right here. And yes, he is."

"Sorry, but Horace is freaking out over here." Bianca shook her head. "He's babbling something about how Fred bringing you there will make big giant trouble."

"Good." Fred slammed a metal locker shut. He slung a huge canvas sack across his body. "Trouble of the biggest, most giant variety is exactly what I want to bring. She took Ed, Bianca."

"She—" Bianca tilted her head, as though listening to something Fred and I couldn't hear. "Great Ghostly Realm, you don't mean the king's opposite?"

"What, you can't even say the Sidhe Queen here or something?" I put my hands over my mouth a moment later. All the levitating objects in the room dropped.

"No. No, you can't." Fred sighed, shoulders drooping as if

something a hundred times heavier than his bag dragged at them. He gestured at the stairs. "Ladies first."

"I just played our outro on accident, huh?" I walked up, not bothering to glance over my shoulder to see if Fred heard me.

"Pretty much." A chuckle bubbled up from his throat, oddly melodic. "It's a good thing. Bianca's one of those people it's easy to lose track of time while talking to."

"Oh." I wasn't sure why that bothered me. I shouldn't care who Fred Redford liked talking to. We'd reached the door to the steps leading down to the old trolley tunnel, so I got a chance to look at his face. "Maybe you should take her out for coffee sometime."

"Um, no." Fred headed down the stairs before I could meet his eyes, but too late to hide his blanching face.

"I expected more blushing from a lunk like you," I teased as I followed him down. "Instead, you went paler than a vampire."

"I don't date." He opened the door and let me through, but his hand closed around my upper arm before I could head back out to Thayer Street. "The gate to the Under is back through here."

"Wow, kinda biased of your school to put their Nocturnal Lounge here." I walked behind him through the dark, gloomy tunnel.

"Not really."

"Well, it seems like it, being right next to the lounge the Unseelies and undead use." My motocross boots crunched in some kind of gravel or grit before Fred stopped. "Makes things super easy."

"You have no idea, do you?" Fred turned to face me, then leaned against the concrete wall. "Headmistress Thurston walks a fine line between the Courts. She's on a first-name basis with both my dad and Hertha Harcourt, who's one of the queen's biggest allies here in Rhode Island. You're the one being biased, anyway."

"What's that supposed to mean?" I held my head high, instantly on the defensive.

"You see the Nocturnal Lounge and the nearest gate to it and make assumptions." Fred snorted. "I bet you haven't even set foot on campus. Do you have any idea how much bigger and closer to everything the Solarium is? Did you bother asking me to tell you that their Under Gate's right inside their lounge? Of course not. You just saw one side and judged. Definition of bias if I ever heard one."

"Oh." I didn't back down physically, but the lunk had a point. "Look, I'm sorry. It's just that it makes me nervous, seeing an imbalance with anything faerie."

"Why?" Fred's one-word question was almost a whisper.

"What's it to you?" I peered up at Fred, trying to read his expression. I might have pushed him too far with the ribbing. Regular plain old human eyes didn't adjust to darkness like a Redcap's. I could have used my Empathy, but that would have felt like cheating.

"We're about to go somewhere a hundred times weirder than ghost vacuum day at the Nocturnal Lounge because I got handed an honest to goodness Quest while I'm still just a changeling. I have no idea why you're even helping me. For all I know, you're a Seelie ally. You have to give me something, or by the Goblin King's Garters, I'm leaving you out here and going it alone."

I froze. It wasn't a question of how much I wanted to tell him, or how much I should. What I could had limits, or I'd be too much of an emotional wreck to help with this task, anyway. I closed my eyes even though I couldn't see him all that well. I knew he could see me perfectly fine after all. For whatever reason, even though I performed for millions of people, I didn't even want an audience of one for this.

"Your brother's not the first child the queen's tried to steal away." All my flesh went goose, telling me I'd barely skirted disaster with my confession. "I can't say much more right now.

Just that I'm helping because Psychic kids don't belong in the Under."

"Fair enough." Fred clicked his tongue against his teeth. "A common goal will do. And for Pete's sake, don't try to talk about it again until whatever Ban's got you lets go, okay?"

"Oh, don't worry." My goosebumps eased back down into a more normal state. I didn't bother telling Fred I wasn't under a faerie Ban, just a regular psychological human one. "I'm used to not talking about plenty of things."

"Good. While we're talking about not talking about things, no more about dating, either." Fred held one hand out toward me in the darkness. "Take it when you're ready. We'll need to hold hands until we're through. And after that, don't go off the path no matter what. Leave anything off to the side to the changeling, *capisce?*"

"*Ponimat'.*" I grinned, knowing he could see me. I wanted our truce back.

"Huh?" I imagined Fred scratching his head.

"It means I understand." I snickered, hoping he'd take it kindly. "If you're going to spice up your English with Mama's Italian, I'm doing the same with Grandpa's Russian. It's only fair."

I waited until he nodded before taking his hand. After that, Fred pulled something from his bag and scraped it across the tunnel wall, marking out a glowing rectangle on the brick surface. The outline's pale shimmer deepened to a red too crimson to be fiery. The wall crumbled away, and we walked through together.

My eyes were open, but the world looked blank. Not black like the tunnel or a room with no light, not the swirls and loops of eyelid interiors. I mean blank like a sheet of paper, but even that's not right since paper is white. The world before my eyes was colorless. I'd expected the deep crimson of Fred's faerie doorway magic but found I shouldn't have.

My right hand was stuck in something up to the wrist. It felt less like what I knew it was, Fred's hand, and more like leather. That was the only thing I could feel by touch, too. I tried looking at him, but my eyes still saw blank everything, and I wasn't even sure my head turned. If I even had a head that was. But no, I still had a head. I could hear, even though my most dependable sense was on the fritz, with something between static and the pressurized cabin of an airplane the only discernible sound.

I reached out with Psychic Empathy, trying to sense that way even though I was more accustomed to broadcasting emotion than opening myself up to it. And that hated last resort worked.

The rest of my senses came back with pins and needles, waking limbs and eyes and ears. The Under wouldn't let me deny who and what I was. I finally understood in practice how it might have been for Bobby if the bear shifter had tried coming here. He'd have been forced into his bear form the same way I'd been forced to see everything through the filter of my Psychic ability. Glancing over at Fred, I understood that the realm of faeries and their kin was an equal opportunity tangle of truth. If I wasn't careful, my figurative demons could go on display for anyone we happened to meet. But mine were nowhere near as blatant as Fred Redford's.

"Sorry." He hung his massive flat-on-top-but-otherwise spiky-haired head. His skin was gray, although not the way the Hollywood makeup artists color the faces of zombies. I remembered that all Redcap changelings who'd used their faerie magic would look like this without a glamour. Fred's skin was something in between two extremes, which made sense since he hadn't tithed. Either it was some vestige of one of Grandpa's stories, or the Under reminding me of the important fact that Fred hadn't chosen a side. He loosened his grip on my hand. "I'm so sorry about how I look. And now you know why I don't date."

"It's okay." I left my hand in his massive one, our palms flat against each other. Fred's fingernails looked more like petrified wood chips. His eyes and lips were red, the former gleaming like Sauron's eye and the latter more stained like the shark in Jaws. His muscles bulged, lumpy and veined like the Hulk's, but more terrifying than incredible. I took a deep breath, the same as I did every time I stepped on a stage or turned on a camera. "I can handle it."

Until the words came out of my mouth, I hadn't realized they were true. Good thing, too. Ed Redford couldn't afford a full-blown Irina Kazynski freak out session. After Fred's remarks about dating or the lack thereof, he couldn't either.

"Thanks." He stood, managing to keep his palm under mine the whole time.

It surprised me how much grace came in such a bulky figure. I'd never expect anyone to understand unless they saw it for themselves. Not many would dare. I could see why Redcaps in stories from before the Reveal got the monstrous villain treatment. But Grandpa always taught me that real evil in the world most often had an all too human face. Also, since our first meeting at the party, I knew better than to judge Fred based on his looks alone.

"So, where do we go from here?" I stood up, balancing with his help despite the vanishing tingles in my feet.

"You know, I'm not sure." Fred scratched his head, which was weird. The Redcap's fingers raked through his hair, where his magical cap should have been. That was twelve kinds of wrong. I'd thought he just glamoured it for all the regular people, but I was wrong.

"*Govno*." I took a deep breath, trying not to jump to a conclusion and panic.

"Is that one of Grandpa's Russian swear words?" The corner of his mouth tilted up in a half-smile.

"Yeah." I wasn't going to translate that one for him. "Fred, we have a huge problem."

"What's that?" He put his hands on his hips.

"This is the Under, so glamour doesn't work here, right?" I had to make sure this wasn't just some kind of paranoid misunderstanding on my part.

"Mostly." Fred nodded.

"What do you mean by mostly?" I tilted my head, peering up at him.

"A pure faerie's glamour still works unless someone or something with stronger magic takes it off. Same goes for a Monarch's." Fred shrugged. "But I'm definitely not either of those."

"Okay. So, new but not unrelated question." I took another deep breath. "You're a Redcap. Doesn't that mean you should always have a cap on?"

"Yeah." He shuddered. "And I don't."

"Bingo."

"Lynn was right." Fred closed his eyes. He didn't have to translate. I knew what that word meant. "*Merde*."

"My sentiments exactly." I dashed behind Fred without looking to see who'd spoken behind me, then peeked out from around one of his massive arms.

A statuesque redheaded woman with a fanged smile stood leaning on a walking stick, her back to the gate from the trolley tunnel. I blinked, wondering how a vampire had managed to open the gate from the other side. changelings and faeries couldn't get turned. It just didn't take. And then, the walking stick moved on its own with a slight creak.

"A vampire with a brownie?" I blinked. "What are you, a Summoner or something?"

"You guessed right. I'm a Psychic vampire." She dimmed down the smile though I could still see her fangs. I hoped she wasn't hungry. "But you still have no idea who I am, though."

"True." Fred shrugged. "So tell us, already."

"Margot Malone." She dropped the name like a gauntlet.

"The reporter?" Fred cracked his knuckles. "You following us for a scoop or something?"

"Maybe," Margot grinned, patting the messenger bag clinging to her right hip. "It's awfully interesting, seeing the accomplished violinist, Irina Kazynski, taking a trip to the Under with a Redcap who just happens to be friends with Lane Meyer, of all people. Do I smell a collaboration in the future?"

"Shouldn't you be writing about WaterFire or a Night Creatures concert instead of barging in here after us?" I stepped to the side of Fred with my hands on my hips, still not quite daring to get in between him and a potentially hungry vampire.

"Was on my way to do exactly that, you know." She shrugged. "Twiggy here helps me get around town in the daytime by taking shortcuts through the Under. I was just kidding about following you for a scoop, although whatever you're doing here would make an excellent piece for my blog if you ever want to tell me about it." Margot brandished a business card at me.

"Not happening." I crossed my arms over my chest.

"I'm about to tithe, so maybe you'll get your story in a year and a day." Fred plucked the card from her hand and pocketed it. "Nice meeting you and all, but we have to get going." Fred turned toward the fork in the path leading south.

"Wait." Margot rummaged in her bag. "If you're going to the queen's demesne on that road, you'll want these." She held out a thin stack of post-it notes.

"Why? What are those?" Fred tilted his head, peering at the paper with one baleful eye.

"Psychic paper." I chuckled. "Wow, Margot. You must really want that story. Technically, I can only see that they're imbued with Psychic energy, not what kind."

"For a woman who chose music over magic, you sure know a

truckload about my world." Fred's mumble was more like a rumble.

"I call these my Summoner hall passes." Margot pushed shook them. "There's only three, but they'll let you call one of my pure faerie friends named on the paper."

"Why?" Fred narrowed his eyes. "What's in it for you?"

"You're friends with Lane Meyer." She flashed us that fanged smile again. I froze. Why were Margot's fangs scarier than Fred's teeth? "I need an interview with him this summer if I want to get assigned to cover the Brodsky Case this fall."

"Listen, Margot." Fred sighed. "You have the wrong idea. I'm probably not coming back from the Under." My stomach felt like Fred had dropped it off a skyscraper without the rest of me. Fred glanced down at me and blinked, then grinned. The falling feeling stopped. "It's time for me to tithe soon."

"But Irina will go back." The vampire nodded at me. "Neither Monarch would dare hold the bearer of that violin. She can give Lane a message for you."

"Will you do that, Irina?" Fred put the decision that'd get us extra help on me. I made a choice. We had to get Ed out of the Under.

"Sure." Interview with the scary vampires it was.

"Then you've got a deal, Margot." He smiled and took the paper. I tried not to smirk as the vampire blinked, her steps shifting nervously as she realized the Redcap's teeth trumped hers by a mile.

She headed down the western fork, raising one arm to wave as she went. We continued to the south, in the direction I could only assume led into the queen's demesne.

"You really think we'll need those, Fred?" I watched him tuck the papers in his pocket.

"We'll need all the help we can get at this point. changelings aren't as powerful as tithed faeries, and without my cap, I'm even more limited." He plodded along until bells rang out in the distance and yet right nearby at the same time. Fred held his head held up as though waiting for something. When the chimes stopped, I understood. "We have eight more of the queen's hours before Ed's stuck in here forever."

"Then let's go!" I picked up the pace, power-walking like women did on the Fenway back up in Boston. Fred caught up, matching my pace with ease. The path was clear, flat, smooth. I couldn't imagine we wouldn't make it in time. I'd forgotten that, technically, this was still Providence. Anywhere we went in the Under would still be Rhode Island because that's where we'd entered from. I'd stopped thinking about my jinx or the Extramagus explanation Fred had tried using to change my mind.

CHAPTER FIVE

Fred

I glanced at my surly traveling companion every so often, still not sure why she was helping me. But I couldn't bring myself to question her motives anymore. Dad always told me worrying won't fix anything. Only action can do that. So, I kept on keeping on. If Irina had her own motives for coming with me, so be it. She'd already saved my life and gotten us the Psychic papers by agreeing to introduce Lane to Margot. I couldn't imagine anyone with a nefarious secret agenda doing stuff like that.

One thing I realized was that, as a Psychic, she didn't experience our surroundings the way I did. She walked as though the path was straight, the terrain flat. It wasn't. I knew, probably because all my senses worked here, that we went at a slight incline. The air started smelling different, salty but without the heavy humidity of ocean I'd grown up with in the regular version of Rhode Island. When I saw a shimmer, more solid than a mirage in summer, worry struck a gasp from me. I stopped walking, hoping the distant glimmer wasn't what I thought it was. Irina took three more steps ahead, then stopped too.

"What's wrong, Fred?" She turned to look back at me, nose wrinkling. "And what's that salt smell?"

"Oh, wow." I nodded, grinning at her. "I get it now. You're nearly blind here in the regular world sense. It's your Empathy that lets you see, so I need to notice something before you do."

"Well, duh." Irina's thumb and pointer finger made the shape of an L on her forehead. She rolled her eyes, surprising me with her casual reaction to being told she couldn't strictly see. "But what about my question?"

"I'm not sure. Even though I've heard stories about this area, but can't be certain if what's up ahead is in them or not." I shrugged. "We'll have to get closer to see without that glare."

"Okay, then let's go." She moved the strap on her bag so it sat on her other shoulder.

"Yeah, sure." I strode forward, one step letting me come even with her.

We walked along in silence for a while as the sun appeared to rise in the sky. I knew that wasn't true, though. Once we got to the heart of the queen's territory, it'd seem like noon no matter what hour the clock said. Fortunately for vampires like Margot, the Under's sun didn't burn them. I wasn't sure why. Maybe ten minutes later, I saw the obstacle, but it was Irina who gasped.

"Oh, no way." She shielded her eyes with one hand but kept walking. "How are we supposed to get past something like that?"

"I don't know." My stomach rumbled. "I guess I could try taking a bite once we get there."

"Are you sure that's a good idea?" She looked up at me, the right corner of her lower lip tilted into her mouth as she chewed on it. "I mean, you haven't been keeping anything down too well today. Not even sandwiches."

"I'll try it anyway." I swallowed, the pesto chicken choking disaster playing out in my mind. "It's what Redcaps do."

"I thought you fixed stuff, built things." Irina glanced at me. "Renovated apartments with enchanted tools."

"Well, we do that, too. Especially out on the other side. But in the Under—" I bared my teeth, gesturing at them. "Well, let's just say we were made for different things. When the monarchs split, we adapted." I hoped she'd just leave it at that.

"When you say different things, what do you mean, exactly?" Irina's Empathy conveyed genuine curiosity behind her words.

"Um, that's a new question." I blinked, unsure why even my closest friends had never asked me this particular one before. Maybe some of them knew already, but I suspected a different reason. "I think most people are afraid to ask."

"What, because you're strong and have big, um, teeth and everything?" She lengthened her stride to keep up with me better. I hadn't realized I'd started walking faster.

"Not really." I slowed my pace. "I mean, think of the scariest fairy tales. What do the worst monsters in those stories do?"

"They—" She put one hand to her cheek, almost like she had trouble contemplating imaginary monsters. Everyone knew Grandpa Kazynski had survived the Holocaust. I wondered how much he'd told Irina. "Oh. They eat people."

"Yeah." My face tightened in a disgusted grimace. "And the main power us Redcaps have is the ability to eat anything."

"So, people are scared of that." Irina snorted. "Well, I think vampires are scarier. They need to drink blood from the living. You can eat anything at all." She grinned. "What's the weirdest thing you ever ate?"

"That I can remember?" I grinned. "A bunch of fireworks."

"Seriously?" She chuckled. "Why?"

"We had a drought the first year fireworks were legal in Rhode Island. Also, a brush fire out near our lake house in Gloucester. I ate the fireworks to help the Fire Department out. Almost went into that instead of engineering, but—" I shrugged.

"Yeah, you got hit with the family business bug." Irina nodded. "I know that feeling all too well."

"Oh, boy." I shuddered, remembering the taste of fireworks.

They'd been nothing like Pop-Rocks. "We're here. And it's worse than I thought."

We gazed together up at what had to be a mile-high wall of solid rock salt. It gleamed in the sunlight like raw quartz, but my nose knew better. The section by the path was seamed with cracks and crevices, none of which looked climbable without equipment.

"Good thing I brought this." I rummaged in my bag until what I wanted came to my hand.

"Um, no." Irina recoiled from the sight of the ropes, hooks, and clasps I'd dropped on the path in front of me. She shivered but seemed to have started sweating at the same time.

"No?" I blinked. Irina seemed so bold, jumping right in with the Heimlich maneuver, banishing my nausea with her music, and daring to come to the Under with only a changeling for company. Cowardly was the last word I'd have thought applied to her.

"No. Way. Jose." She shivered from head to toe, like a southern belle in a blizzard.

Okay, then." I gathered up the climbing gear and stuffed it back in my bag. "We'll find a way through."

She said nothing, but the whoosh of exhaled breath and the slowly easing position of her shoulders told me everything I needed to know. Irina Kazynski was scared to death of heights and couldn't climb the wall. I wasn't sure I had the strength to do it either if I was honest with myself. I walked right up to its bumpy surface, cracked my knuckles, and stretched my neck. Then, I massaged my jaw.

Irina stood back and watched as I opened up and took the biggest bite I could out of the wall. Imagine having your mouth full of rock candy. Now imagine those jagged points of sweetness are salt. That's what it was like. My teeth made short work of the crystals. After all, even rock salt isn't as hard to chew as rocks and minerals. I breathed a sigh of relief that it wasn't quartz or amethyst instead. When I spun on my heel and gave Irina a thumbs-up, I had no idea it'd be a mistake.

My gut contracted, and my throat opened right back up again. I made it to the edge of the path before losing everything in my stomach. Then I laid there, face against gravel that matched the wall in color if not composition. The smell just made everything worse.

"Fred, you okay?" Irina sat beside me, holding my wrists. Her thumbs pressed against them, not like taking a pulse, but between the tendons on the undersides of them. Pressure points.

"Yeah." I lied. Even though the acupressure she'd done helped a little, I was still leagues away from okay. "Gonna try something else in a minute."

But it took less time than that. Maybe it was her Empathy, but whatever spot Irina pressed in my wrists made my stomach stop heaving. I sat up faster than I thought I'd be able to, then rummaged in my pack again, with both hands this time. The weight of the two things I pulled out felt unfamiliar, yet I knew that in the Under, my body would sense how to use them. They were tools, and part of the new nature of Redcaps was fixing things.

"You're attacking the wall?" Irina stood back to give me plenty of room. "With giant monkey wrenches?"

"You can call it that if you want." I grinned. "Technically, I'm renovating. Making a new door. Just watch me!"

I rushed the wall just like the guys in Kung-Fu movies flew at an opponent, pinwheeling my arms on the way for extra momentum. Right up until the first wrench made its impact, I kept the idea in my head that rock salt would shatter and spray out like hail. Sometimes, things in the Under reacted the way you believed they would, but not this time. I was wrong.

My elbow and shoulder jarred at the impact, the latter popping dangerously close to dislocation. I'd done that before and didn't want a repeat performance, thank you very much.

The second wrench hit with a clang. I almost praised the Goblin King when I heard the pattering aftermath of something in tiny bits dropping to the ground. But it wasn't the wall that broke.

I stared down at what remained of the wrench handle in my left hand, then looked back at the wall. The only mark on it had come from my teeth, which were, after all, sharp enough to cut diamonds when I needed them to be.

"Oh, no!" Irina whisked a bandanna out of her bag, then brushed by me to sweep up the shards of my dearly-departed wrench. "Iron bad, right?"

"Well yeah, but that's not iron." I sighed, my shoulders drooping. "It's a titanium alloy. I wouldn't be able to work with iron tools."

"I should have known." She got up, a sigh to match her freshly crossed arms escaping her lips. "Well, now what?"

"I've got something else in here that might do the trick." I fumbled around in my bag again after replacing the one wrench. The thing I pulled out, this time, looked like the corner of your vision.

"What's that?"

"Portable hole." I held it up gingerly. "Gotta handle it carefully because if I drop it, there'll be a pit in the path, and we don't want that."

"I'll believe it when I see it." She rolled her eyes.

"Me, too," I smirked. This had to work.

I stepped right up to the wall, held up the portable hole, and tried to apply it like plaster under the spot I'd bitten. It didn't stick. I tried the bitten chunk. No dice. I figured the third time would be the charm, so I pressed it on again, gliding my hands to smooth it against the bumpy surface closest to the path. It flopped in, folding over and disappearing as it fell inside itself.

"Don't believe it." She raised an eyebrow.

"You can't believe everything you see in the Under." I rubbed my chin. "I guess you can't technically see everything you believe, either."

"Wow, you sound like a Redcap fortune cookie." She shook her head, blinking as though she couldn't believe she was actually in the Under and stuck in front of an impassible salt wall. I didn't blame her. I could barely believe it myself, and I'd been raised to expect it.

"So, what now?" I closed up my pack.

"You're asking me?" Irina blinked.

"Yeah." I tapped the side of my head. "My thinker needs to dangle some carrots over the hamster up there until it starts running again."

Irina did the last thing I expected. She threw back her head and laughed. I hadn't even seen her give a full-on smile the entire time I'd known her, and here she was, busting her gut over the lamest joke ever made in either realm.

I blinked, then scratched my head. And then I started laughing. Couldn't help it because that Psychic Empathy of hers made it virally infectious. It was almost like magic. If this was how her Empathy affected any sound she made and applied it to, I could understand why she'd chosen a music school over magical education. Almost. Our mingled voices came back to us, returned by the obstacle the Sidhe queen had surely put in our way on purpose. They sounded louder, more melodic, stronger somehow.

"Hey, Fred." She took a deep breath, recovering from our literal roll on the floor laugh-fest. "You tell that hamster to take a nap. I think I know exactly what to do."

Irina opened her bag and took out her violin case. She set it on the path and leaned down to open it, then held her instrument and bow at the ready. After that, she waited until she caught my eye and winked.

When her bow drew across the strings, notes poured out like before through her kitchen window. Here in the Under, they were actually nearly visible. They made wakes through the air, or maybe it was better to say seeing the music was like watching heat shimmer up from blacktop on a hundred-degree day.

And the wall sang back at her. It all made sense. Crystals resonated with frequencies, and this rock salt barricade was no different. The sound return wasn't an echo this time, more like reverb on an electric instrument. Or maybe not. It was more than that, somehow fuller. But it still sounded and felt only almost right.

Irina stopped playing, socking the violin against her hip and tapping the bow against the calf of her boot. She chewed her lip under a furrowed brow, her eyes shifting to the right as she peered at nothing in particular.

"Something's missing," she finally said. "But what?"

"Do you know *Free Bird?*" I grinned up at her, sure I had the other half of our solution.

"Are you kidding me?" Irina's cheeks colored, probably with anger. She had a temper almost as high as my Mama's.

"A little, sorry." I shook my head. "Why not try playing something that has words so I can help? We laughed together, so maybe the music needs to be a duet, too."

She blinked, shook her head, rolled her eyes. I sat, gazing up at her, waiting for some verbal response.

CHAPTER SIX

Irina

"You? Carry a tune?" I tried not to laugh. I couldn't imagine a lunk like Fred being able to sing, no matter how nice a tone and timbre his speaking voice had.

"What makes you think I can't?" He stood, brushing off his hands.

"Look at you." I did, letting my gaze traveled up and down, then across his bulky frame.

"Yeah, and?" Fred looked down at the path, shifting his weight from one foot to the other. He looked a little pale, too. Maybe that was from trying to eat a hunk of salt earlier.

"Someone your size must spend half the day working out. No time to practice up to anything like a decent level." I sighed, wishing he could somehow pull it off. It'd figure the wall wanted a concert. "I'm not saying it's a bad thing, just not what we need right now."

"You know what they say about the word assume, right? Makes an ass out of you and me." Fred grinned. "I'm big because my dad owns a contracting company. Started working for him seven years ago. Tony Gitano and Lane Meyer work with me. We help Lane practice all his cover songs. So what do you say? Give a lunk a chance."

"Only one way I'll do that." I raised an eyebrow, wondering whether he'd be able to accept my terms. Most guys like him I'd met only knew a few songs.

"Anything." He smiled.

"No *Free Bird*, no *Wayward Son*, no *Stairway to Heaven*." I tapped my foot, waiting for his acceptance or denial.

"No classic rock?" He actually pouted. "It's the genre I know the most lyrics to."

"Well, I didn't say no classic rock, just not those particular songs." I set my instrument under my chin. "Look, I have an idea." I took up my bow and set it on the strings. "Let's just give it a whirl and see if we can do this."

I funneled Empathy at Fred, hoping he'd recognize and know the song. Lots of people didn't until I played the vocal melody. But those pointy Redcap changeling ears of his must have been better than regular plain old human ones. Either that or my own powers were stronger in the Under. Notes bounced off the wall for a few bars, then Fred sang my favorite old song by The Doors.

He sang the line about how day and night divide each other with spot-on pitch, which surprised me. I stopped myself from wondering whether Fred had chosen magic over music, the inverse of my own decision. Instead, I listened to the reverb echoing off the giant wall in our way. After that, he gave me a smirk to shame Alan Rickman and tweaked some lyrics.

"Tried to eat, tried to climb," Fred took a deep breath, then belted out the start of the chorus to *Break On Through*.

When he repeated the lyric, the ground shook as a thin black jagged line formed in the middle of the wall. The third time he sang it, the crack widened. We kept playing, our combined effort inspiring more zig-zag breaches in the barrier formerly known as rock-solid. I skipped the bridge because I never liked playing it, anyway. Fred took it in stride, recognizing the changes I'd made as easily as I adapted to his lyrical improv.

When Fred sang about how straight, deep, and wide the gate was, he held his arms at his sides, hands in fists. He stomped his right foot, then belted out "break on through to the other side!"

The section of wall blocking the path fell, but not in some kind of avalanche down and out toward us. Instead, the rubble rolled away, down to the last pebble. I felt a surge of skittering terror, alien and inanimate as though the broken bits of that barrier feared our combined efforts.

At the end of the song, Fred laughed. He turned around and gave me two thumbs up, smiling away with those jagged Redcap teeth. I raised the bow to my forehead, saluting with my instrument like Grandpa always said the trumpeter on the tower of Krakow in Poland did. I packed the violin back in its case, pausing to trace the seal of the Goblin King. It made me wonder something.

"Hey, Fred?" I closed and latched the case, keeping my back to him. "When you're done getting your brother back, you'll be in the middle of the queen's territory."

"Yeah, that's right." He cleared his throat. Not the way people do when they have more to say, but when they want to change the subject. I didn't let him.

"And you said before that you won't be able to get out of the Under again." I tucked the case into my satchel. "So how are you going to get to the king's demesne in time to tithe to him?"

"Irina, look at me," Fred whispered.

I stood before turning. Shouldn't have. Fred was paler than he'd been before, especially around his lips. His eyes had the beginnings of dark circles under them. The hair at the top of his head looked even spikier and more cockeyed than it had when we came through the gate. I hadn't had a fear of him for even a minute, but now, I feared for him. The drastic change in his appearance hurt my heart almost as much as seeing

Grandpa at the hospital. If Fred looked that bad, how terrible did he feel?

"What do we do now?" I'd chickened out of asking how he was or actually doing anything remotely comforting.

"We go on." He turned his back on the way we'd come and started walking through the gap in the wall.

"Thanks, Captain Obvious." I trotted to catch up to him. "But you didn't answer my question about the king."

"I thought it was way too personal." He stared straight ahead.

"Tough, because you're implying you'll be stuck here. And if that happens, what about Ed and me?"

"The queen's good for her word. She'll let Ed go if I meet her terms." He finally glanced down at me. "And Margot knew what she was talking about. You're carrying that case. Those two seals give you a get out of the Under free card on either side."

"So, what are you going to do, then?"

"Dunno." He shrugged. "Don't care, as long as you guys get out. Probably live the rest of my life in the queen's dungeon if I'm lucky."

"But I thought all changelings have a choice about tithing. Why would you get locked up?"

"This." Fred pointed at his hatless head. "If I don't get my cap back, even my own mother would want me locked up."

"You didn't seem too worried about not having it before we came here." I narrowed my eyes. "What changed?"

"I wasn't sure it was gone. The rest of this talk will have to wait, Irina." Fred stopped on a dime, dropping one of his massive hands on my right shoulder before I could step past him.

A path just big enough for us to walk side by side stretched out in front of us for about a hundred feet, ending in a fork. Along either side, towering above even Fred's head, were more walls. The barrier appeared to be stalks of young, green bamboo, but appearances weren't everything. Fred let go of me.

The wind blew gently from the southwest, and a hollow

percussive sound rose musically up ahead. The walls rippled in the breeze. They weren't walls at all. This was a field of bamboo. No, not bamboo. Not in the Under. These were brownies.

"Welcome to the queen's maze." The voice came from ahead and to the left. Before Fred could stop me, I headed to its source and stood, facing its general direction.

"Thanks. I've never been here before." I knew better than to ask one pure faerie a direct question, let alone a whole crop of them.

"We know." A ripple and that hollow wind sound came again, but this time, the air was still.

"You're laughing at us." Fred's shadow merged with mine, then grew until it almost topped the wall. "Not a nice way to treat guests."

"It tickles, having people in the maze," said the voice. "It's better than butterflies."

"We won't be long," I grinned, singling out the brownie who'd spoken as a stalk with a peculiar vertical beige streak which set them apart from the others. "We're on our way to the queen's castle."

"You won't be long through this younger half of the maze where we still have roots. But the older side's another story. I bet you want to ask how to get through their side."

"It's not up to me." I shook my head. "This is Fred's Quest."

"Yeah," Fred grumbled. "You don't want to make me angry, especially since I lost my cap."

"That's right." Stalks swayed and bent. "And we won't. We're just giving you a warning, so don't eat the messengers."

"Fine, I don't much like string beans, anyway. And thanks for the heads up." Fred's shadow withdrew, leaving mine alone. "Come on, Irina. I know how to get through this maze."

I turned to follow him, still intrigued by the brownie who'd spoken. I wasn't sure why, if it was young, it had such a horrible scar. Who would maim a defenseless rooted brownie? I wasn't a fan of faerie, but couldn't deny my soft spot for anything in distress. It's part of Psychic Empathy, and one reason most of my performances got recorded and uploaded instead of gigged out in public.

Fred took a piece of chalk out of his bag, the kind he'd used to mark the walls back at Grandpa's apartment and make the door to the Under. He couldn't mark the path. It was coarse gravel all through here. Instead, he gently marked a brownie.

"Tickles!" The brownie's voice sounded high-pitched and breathless. "Hee!"

"See?" Fred grinned. "Piece of cake." He must have actually imagined eating cake because he blanched.

"You okay?" I put out an arm to steady him.

"Yeah, just gotta keep my head in the game and out of the bakery case," Fred smirked. "I won't hurl again. Nothing left in there anyway." He patted his stomach. "Let's try the right side first, okay?"

"Sure." I reached out one bent arm, hoping he'd take the hint. He did, offering his. I looped mine through, and we walked together. Neither of us wanted to lose the other in there.

Every time we came to a fork, Fred marked another brownie. Every one of them giggled. Some of their neighbors begged to be tickled, too, and Fred did, just not with the chalk. Whenever we got to a dead end, retracing from the marks he'd left was easy. With the childlike brownie laughter and Fred taking his time and treating the maze like a puzzle, we almost had fun.

Eventually, we came to the middle the brownies had mentioned. Fred sat down on a stone bench to rest, facing toward a huge fountain shaped like a tree at the center. He put the chalk back in his bag and rummaged again, coming up with a thermos.

"What's that?" I eyed the container warily, worried that whatever it was would only make Fred sick.

"Just water." He opened it and poured some in the lid. "Want some?"

"Thanks." I reached out and took a sip, then another. He refilled my cup before taking a swig himself.

"By the way, don't drink any of that." He pointed at the fountain with the container.

"No?" I peered at the fine spray coming from the undersides of the stone branches. "Looks safe enough, but something feels off about it."

"Yeah. Look down there." He gestured at the ground.

"Oh." I saw that the path ran around the fountain, but didn't go all the way up to it. A two-foot wide section of tall grass separated it from us. "If I stepped on that, I'd go off the path."

"Right." Fred leaned the thermos on his knee. "You've got a good instinct for this magic stuff, despite choosing music instead."

"Thanks, I guess." I couldn't look at him all of a sudden. "I could say the same for you about music. You've got pipes and pitch."

"Yeah. I chose magic."

"Funny how we both ended up in the same place despite taking opposite paths. Life's kind of like a maze sometimes, don't you think?"

"Yeah, kind of like a giant labyrinth. Not really so funny, though." His sigh weighed so much I turned to look at him again. "I told you, it's coincidence. That Extramagus. And maybe something else."

"What do you mean?"

"You asked about my cap earlier." Fred shook his head. "Every faerie has a weakness. For a Redcap, it's our red caps, of course. Without it, it's only a matter of time before I lose all my marbles."

"And there's no way to stop it?"

"I could get my cap back. But there's just about no chance of that happening. It'd take a miracle."

"Why? Don't you know how you lost it?"

"Yeah." Fred looked down at the ground.

"So, you should be able to get it back then, eventually." I shook out the now empty thermos lid.

"I lost it out there," Fred waved his hand back to the north, "not here in the Under. And I can't go back for a year and a day. By then, it'll be too late, even if I tithe. My sanity will be gone forever."

"There has to be something we can do." I handed him the lid. "I can go get it for you. Margot mentioned I could travel with the seals in my violin case."

"Yeah, you could. But you won't be able to get my cap back." Fred held the lid in his hand, then tilted the thermos back and killed its contents. "Someone took it, you see."

"The Extramagus?" I shuddered.

"Worse." Fred cleared his throat.

"What could be worse than that?"

"Someone I thought was a friend." He spoke so quietly, I almost couldn't hear him.

"Ah."

"Look, I'm pretty much okay with being stuck here. I probably won't know the difference once I go off the deep end, anyway. Whichever Monarch has me can either lock me up or sic me on their enemies for all I'd know." Fred put the lid back on the thermos and stuffed it back in his bag. "But I need two things to happen. Will you help me?"

"I'm already helping you." I reached out intending to pat his hand, but chickened out and flipped my hair over my shoulder instead. "But I'm jinxed, remember?"

"We both are as far as I'm concerned, so it's a wash, anyway." He shrugged.

"Fine." I crossed my arms over my chest. "Tell me about these two things."

"Okay, then." Fred folded his hands together. I noticed how

his left thumb sat on top of his right. "Ed. I need him out of here. And after that, I need you to go back and find my friends. Find Josh Dennison, or Bobby, or Blaine Harcourt. And you tell them not to trust Tony Gitano. Don't tell them in front of Jeannie or Ismail because then they won't believe you. Same goes for Henry Baxter."

"I'll do it." I nodded.

"I need you to promise." Fred lowered his head, staring into my eyes.

"I promise, Fred." I stared back, unblinking. "If you lose it, I'll make sure Ed's safe. I'll tell Josh, Bobby, or Blaine about Tony."

"Thanks." Fred took the chalk out of his bag again. "Let's move on, then."

We stood, following the path as it circled around the fountain. On the other side, opposite from the way we came, was another opening into a path lined with more brownies. These were tinted yellow-brown instead of green. I took a deep breath and followed Fred into the second half of the maze.

CHAPTER SEVEN

Fred

I side-eyed this new set of brownies. When the wind blew, they moved more, and the noise they made clacking against each other sounded louder, more like the bamboo wind chimes in our garden. Still, I chalk marked them just like the younger, green ones, even though they didn't giggle until we'd passed them by. I stuck to my previous strategy, marking near corners so we'd be able to backtrack accurately.

Except it didn't work.

I didn't notice until we'd tried retracing our steps twice. Losing my cap had given my mind a keen-edged sort of focus, like tunnel vision. And getting through the maze was the one thing on my mind at that point. I noticed pretty quickly under the circumstances, but not soon enough to salvage the situation. I sat down in the middle of the path, hurling my chalk off into a stand of snickering brownies. Then, I almost got sick again because that reminded me of the Snickers brownies Mama made around Halloween.

"What's up?" Irina stepped around in front of me after

glancing back over her shoulder at the chalk. The brownies closed ranks. No way we'd get it back even if it would have helped.

"We're lost. The marked ones keep moving, and I can't remember how to get back to the middle or think of a different strategy to find a way through."

"Time to phone a friend, maybe?"

"That'd be great and all, Irina, but we don't get cell or satellite reception in the Under." That wasn't technically true, but I wasn't about to explain how djinn magic worked since I wasn't one and couldn't use it anyway. I made a fist and punched the ground.

"Hall passes, Fred. The ones that vampiric cross between Lois Lane and Mary Jane Watson gave us." She hunkered down, looking me in the face as though she was stupid, fearless, or had nothing to lose. Maybe all three. "We can call one of the creatures on those Psychic paper sticky notes."

"Huh?" I blinked, shook my head. Mistake. That made my stomach churn even worse than before.

"These." Irina reached out, under the Hawaiian shirt I wore over my tee. Her hand dipped into the pocket there, over my heart. I blinked at the sudden softening of my attitude. She brandished a thin stack of square yellow paper.

My mouth dropped open. I'd completely forgotten about Margot and our favor exchange in the maddening focus of trying to solve a rigged maze. I reached to take the papers from Irina but stopped. Maybe I wasn't quite right in the head already.

"Anything there look useful in this situation?"

"Let's see." She peered at the first one. "Pixie. Not helpful here." She hummed, trying to peel the first sheet back to get a look at the second. "Hey, a Spite. That'd work."

"Woah, that's maybe not such a good idea." I shuddered. Besides the magic drain, Spites were scary looking and reputedly ferocious. Any creature twisted and warped by faerie magic as a form of punishment should be.

"Why not?" Irina shrugged. "I mean, Spites are the queen's hunting hounds. One of those could sniff their way through a maze like this, right?"

"Yeah, but they also eat magic." I shuddered. "One of them tried hunting down some magical friends of mine. Took literal Luck for them to get away unscathed.

"Good thing I'm a Psychic, then." She grinned.

"Well, but I'm not." I gulped. "With my cap gone, my magic's all over the place."

"All over the place how, exactly?" Irina's lips curved into a bemused little smile.

"I mean, that's part of what's making me sick. I'm getting severe magic surges, kind of like seizures in my energy field. It happens to changelings when it's almost time for us to come here and tithe, but without my cap, it's even worse, and I can't control it."

"So, it's like feedback from an amp and a microphone being too close together?" She actually smiled.

"Yeah, you got it." I gulped, wondering what had the wheels in her head turning like that.

"Well, one way to get rid of feedback is to turn the volume down somewhere." Irina chewed her lower lip, something I recognized as a habit of hers when she just about had something puzzled out. "I'm calling up the Spite. They're the best choice for more than one reason."

"But what if a super ravenous one comes? It'll leave me stuck here out cold."

"Listen, lunkhead. I'm an Empath, and this is Psychic paper. I'll put out vibes so the Spite grabs some magic grub on the way over if that'll chill you out, okay?"

"You can do that?" I blinked, not sure how to process her idea or what to do about it if I could.

"Yeah, sure." Irina turned her back elbows rising as she peeled off the sticky Psychic note that'd summon Margot's Spite.

For the first time, I wasn't sure I believed her. She'd chosen music over magic after all. But it was too late to argue. I watched her shoulders rise and fall five times, some kind of deep breathing exercise, probably. Most Psychics used those. I waited, wondering whether Margot's Spite knew the one who'd hunted Henry and Maddie months ago, or whether they cared that I was a friend and packmate to people who freed one of their kind from the twisted horror of their punishment.

They appeared at the edge of the path, brownies parting to let them through. I knew the spikes on their back used to be wings, which just made the Spite more frightening to look at. Their build went beyond lean to emaciated, ribs and the points of their hips and shoulders looking nearly as sharp as those spikes. And then, they sat at Irina's feet, a long, bruise-yellow tongue lolling from their mouth as they grinned up at her like they had delusions of being the most horrifying Labrador Retriever ever.

I didn't move until they broke eye contact with Irina, and that was just to breathe a sigh of relief as they looked away from me and down the path. The Spite trotted to a fork and faced left, leaving their nearly skeletal tail poking back around the corner, low like an English Pointer.

"Daryl here is going to lead us through." Irina turned and held a hand down to me.

"Daryl?" I blinked up at the woman, not taking her hand. Yet.

"Well, I have to call them something besides 'hey you' or 'poor thing,' don't I?" Irina tilted her head, piercing glare coating over with velvet as she softened her gaze. "And that's what they say they want me to call them. They're helping us because they want to. All the paper does is require a Spite Margot has a contract with to show up. Did you know that?"

"No, not really." The corners of my eyes stung. Even Henry hadn't gotten the name of the Spite he'd met until they were freed and back to being a regular, if heartrendingly maimed, Sprite. And here, this Psychic mortal girl who'd turned her back on the magical world for reasons she refused to discuss, had. I was supposed to be a good guy. So I had to step up. I took her hand. "Thanks."

"Don't mention it." She pulled on my arm. I left enough of a drag to let her think she actually helped me stand up. After that, I walked along slightly behind her as she followed our unlikely guide.

Daryl the Spite trotted through the maze with utter confidence. The brownies edged back from the path, leaving a margin of bare umber ground on either side. None of them wanted to even risk touching a Spite. Draining too much magic from a pure faerie would kill it outright. A Magus or a changeling like me would end up with no magic or possibility of recovering it. And a tithed faerie like my dad would turn mortal, only retaining any Magus powers he might have had. The king's hounds just chased what they hunted to the point of exhaustion. The queen's were much crueler, like their mistress was supposed to be.

"Look how scared they all are of them." I tapped Irina's shoulder. "I've never seen anything like it."

"All that fear just because Daryl's being themself and minding their own business." She shook her head, then raised a hand to one eye. She wiped it. "It must be lonely, being reacted to like that."

"Hey, now it's my turn to ask you what's wrong."

"So go ahead and ask, then."

"Thought I was." I scratched my head, putting on a show in the hopes of cheering her up a little. "Asking, that is."

"Nope. You didn't ask one single thing, lunkhead Fred."

"Okay, so what's wrong, Irina?"

"Daryl can't help being what they are." She gripped the strap on her bag with both hands, squeezing tightly. "Once upon a time, they made a mistake. Probably just one, maybe not something that seemed like such a big deal at the time. And now, Daryl is this. Everything here except the queen, a Redcap on a Quest, and a Psychic who can't even leave the path is scared to death of them. Scared enough to kill."

"Kill? Really? If that's true, why aren't they attacking, do you think?" I stared at Irina's hands, watching the knuckles whiten. "I mean, they outnumber Daryl big time."

"Because we're here. They're either not able or not allowed to do anything directly against us."

"You're probably right. I don't know much about the queen that doesn't come with a lot of crude words." I looked ahead.

Daryl stood in their English Pointer pose again, nose directed at one corner. They moved ahead as we caught up. I saw the exit of the maze at the end of one final straight passageway. We followed the Spite all the way out to where another stone bench squatted on the path like a pair of concrete toadstools under a marble slab.

I sat down to rest, feeling drained but not sick anymore, at least. Maybe Irina had been right, and Daryl's presence got rid of the magic surges because I'd gotten a little hungry. A rummage in my bag brought out a bunch of bananas. Just for kicks, I tried eating one with the peel on. It stayed down. I unhinged my jaw and tossed the rest of the bunch in.

Irina thanked Daryl as I chewed. She even patted them on the head, sending their tail and hips shimmying in a wag more frenzied than the drunkest bridesmaid ever to do the Macarena after multiple sour apple martinis. Daryl tilted their head, yipped three times, and vanished into the underbrush at the edge of the clearing, mostly taken up by a wide spot in the path.

"This is the queen's game." Irina watched the motion of Daryl's passage with shinier than usual eyes. "She's calling the shots here. I just wish I could figure out why."

"That makes two of us." I pulled a sack of apples out of my bag, polished one on my shirt, then handed it to Irina. She sat next to me and took a bite, then jumped at the sound of a voice.

"Did I hear someone say wish?"

We both looked around, not seeing anything or anyone. The voice didn't sound like a brownie from the maze, either.

"Who's there?" I tilted my head, wiggling one of my ears to try to track the voice's direction.

"Henry calls me Sparky." The voice came from above us. I looked up.

A Sprite peered down at me from what looked like a window in the sky. The creature hung from autumnal branches against a wall, blue as that season's skies, with the tattered remnants of its maimed wings straggling out behind them. Sparky used to be a Spite until my friend Nox broke the enchantment on them. I felt Irina tremble at my side and turned to see her looking up with pallid cheeks and eyes focused either inward or on some past event. The apple dropped from her hand, rolling lopsidedly off the path until it came to rest against a gnarled root, bitten side up.

"Uh, hang on, Sparky." I turned to Irina, picking up the hand the apple had occupied a moment before. "It's okay. I know this Sprite. They're bound to a djinn lamp now."

"Oh?" Her voice was farther off than her eyes, tiny. "I know this Sprite, too."

"Yes. I'm glad you remember me." Sparky grinned. "Thank you for being so kind to my friend Daryl. They've been like that for ages, and you're right—it's lonely. I think we're meeting under better circumstances this time."

"Really?" Irina's laugh sounded mechanical, almost a dead sound, like bare branches creaking against a window. "That's not saying much."

"There's hope for your Quest, though." The trees behind Sparky disappeared. "Look."

Sparky the Sprite faded into near transparency, and the sky behind them lit up like a movie screen. A courtyard hewn from golden rock appeared, a round stone table under a tree at the center. I'd seen a replica of that same tree in the fountain at the maze's center. It had to be important.

Beside that on a dais sat a throne encrusted with crystals that caught the light of the noonday sun. An amber-haired woman lay across it, her golden dress draped along her body in a shimmer like dragonfly wings. Sparky had given us a view of the Sidhe queen herself. But I only cared about the person at her feet.

"Ed!" I stood, dropping Irina's hand. I only faintly noticed the slight stickiness of the old apple.

"He can't hear you," Sparky whispered. "Listen." I took the Sprite's advice.

"What do you see him doing now, youngling?" The queen sounded bored, almost tired. But even with the way she reclined in her throne, I could tell it her tone was an act.

"I told you, Majesty, I can't see him doing anything."

"Technicalities, Edward, my boy."

"Not your boy, your Majesty."

"You will be." Her voice reminded me of the time I'd seen a sleepy lioness purring at the zoo. That was right before it pounced on an unfortunate squirrel. "Your usefulness now determines how I treat you later."

"I don't care how you treat me, Majesty."

"Ah, but your brother will. Your mother, too." She shook her head. "And your father. He might even try going to war over how you're treated here, you know."

"Not fair." Ed's shoulders drooped. When he spoke again, I knew it was at least as much an act as the queen's posture. "Your ghosts don't like talking to me, Majesty."

"I don't care, and they know it. Now talk to them and find out what my suitor is doing like a good boy unless you want me to treat you like a delinquent instead."

Ed just nodded, then stared off toward the empty stone table. Well, that's not really true. I knew his gaze met a ghost's, one I couldn't see. I leaned toward Irina, whispered a reminder that Ed was a Medium.

"Majesty," Ed said after a few moments, "Kasa says the guy is in Providence, looking for something."

"Interesting." One of the queen's slipper-clad feet bounced. "What does he seek?"

"A hat."

"Don't lie to me, Edward."

"All right. A cap." Ed blinked a few times, his hands balled up in fists, and his cheeks red. My kid brother was on the verge of tears, but he swallowed them. "My brother's cap."

The left side of the queen's lips tilted up in a smirk. Then she put the fingertips of one hand over her mouth and laughed. It sounded weirdly like a belly-laugh from a woman who'd appear to be yawning if we couldn't hear her. After she had stopped, I watched her shoulders rise as she took a deep breath.

"You see?" She leaned forward, peering at Ed. "Frederick's never getting here in time. Looks like you'll be staying to serve me a nice long while."

"Um, your Majesty?" Ed tilted his head, as though a ghost whispered something in his ear. "We're being watched."

As the queen's eyes narrowed, the entire scene swept away like a kite with a snapped string in a hurricane. Irina let out a long, slow breath. Another deeper exhale matched hers before I realized it was mine. The Sprite reappeared in its illusory autumn trees.

"My debt to you is paid, Irina Kazynski." Sparky's voice faded as they spoke. The window above us dimmed, then vanished entirely.

"Well, now we know why the queen took Ed." I scratched my head. "She's using him to spy on this suitor of hers."

"I wonder why she's got one of those, anyway." Irina shook her head. "What a mess, especially since the entire magical world knows the king's her destiny until one of them dies. And that's not likely to happen. I just don't get it."

"Me neither." I tapped the top of my head. "Maybe it's a fake-out, a manipulative way to send some powerful courtier out to get my cap."

"Okay, let's pretend for a minute she's flirting to get what she wants instead of using the authority of being the Seelie freaking Queen." Irina sat up straighter, swinging her feet under the bench. "Why would she need to send out a faerie to get your cap if you think Tony already took it for her?"

My mouth opened and closed like a fish. I blinked, shrugged, scratched my head. Then I put my hands on my knees before moving them to my temples to start massaging. I felt worlds better than I had back in the maze, for reasons that had nothing to do with magic.

"No clue," I grinned. "But this might be good. Maybe Tony's not a backstabbing jerkface after all."

"Maybe." Irina stretched. "But regardless, we ought to get moving."

As we stood, the clock chimed again. One more hour was gone, and the jungle surrounding the path looked endless.

CHAPTER EIGHT

Irina

"Welcome to the jungle," I said over the eighth and final chime. "Oh, no. We only have five hours now?"

"The wall and the maze must have taken more time than I thought." Fred headed down the path, his strides twice as long as they'd been before and during our time in the maze. "Come on, let's go."

I jogged to keep up, my stomach sinking as I glanced around at the underbrush. It was all fine and well for Daryl the Spite to roam around a jungle in the Under, for me not so much. Fred's words when we entered the Under pounded through my brain along with my hurried footsteps: "Stay on the path." Damn skippy, I'd stay on the path. Wild brownies couldn't drag me away.

Fred glanced over his shoulder, adjusting his stride so I could keep up with him better. I nodded, unable to even give him a breathless word of thanks by that point. I understood the need to hurry, agreed with it, too. The sun in the vision of the queen's courtyard stood at high noon. The sun at the portal had been early dawn. Here, it looked to stand maybe at seven. I'd heard that it didn't move here and you could chart a course by it. We could be as much as an hour behind where we needed to be in order to save Ed. The queen's threats and cruel words still twisted in my gut, driving me even harder to rescue the kid from her clutches at any cost. I shivered.

"It's a jungle, Irina." Fred gave me a look that could have gone from a security guard to a shoplifter. "Subtropical. Why are you shivering?"

"Seeing that woman, how she treated your brother. The queen's just awful." I wasn't about to give him even the short version of a story I'd only ever told to Grandpa, especially not here.

"Yeah. Not what I expected from what I heard growing up, though." He scratched his head. "She's supposed to follow the rules. Faeries aren't supposed to take mortals to the Under without their express agreement. So how and why did she manage to get Ed in the first place?"

"Probably told him she had you here, or your mom or dad." I slapped a hand over my mouth. The last thing Fred needed was more to worry about. If I kept spouting off like that, he'd start asking questions about my past again.

"But she can't lie if she's asked a direct question. Ed knows better than to take any Seelie's word about something like that." He turned on those suspicious eyes again. "Why did you smack yourself?"

"Um." I gulped. "Flies like the jungle. Anyway, she can tell as many half-truths as she wants. That's probably what she did. Made it seem like she had someone Ed cares about here, or maybe made a threat. She has no problem making those as we got to see."

"She sucks." He shook his head.

"Yeah, that she does." I shuddered again but wasn't sure why. I thought I'd pushed the past out of my mind. But I felt hot and cold all at the same time, anyway. Something else had to be going on.

"Hey, what's that smell?" Fred slowed down and looked around. I stopped, too, copying him. When in the Under, do as the changelings do.

The trees hanging over the path blinked with what I thought were eyes at first. Then, I wondered whether they were Christmas lights. They weren't. Instead, flickering flowers in colors like eyes peeked out from under half-moon shaped leaves. I should have had the feeling of being watched. Instead, a far-off scent came, something that seemed familiar. I breathed it in, still unable to place it. It was literally and figuratively at the tip of my nose, causing such an acute sense of curiosity that I kept on sniffing like a mongrel at a dog show.

The flowers started to remind me of eyes again, so I looked over my shoulder. What I saw made me turn right back around and run headlong down the path past Fred. It was some kind of prehistoric cat, or maybe not. Maybe it was something worse, like a saber-toothed horse but way bigger. I didn't want to look back and risk it catching me to find out.

Fred's heavier footsteps pounded up, pacing me. I wondered why he didn't just go ahead of me, but I wasn't sure turning to look at him was a good idea, so I didn't. I just pushed myself and ran even faster. Fred, of course, kept up. This time, I dared a glance at him. His eyes were wide, and his skin was a paler gray than I'd seen it so far, even after he'd lost the battle to keep the rock salt down. He sped up, pulling a few steps past me.

Air stabbed into my lungs as I tried to move my legs faster. If I'd been a singer instead of a fiddler, maybe I would have been in better shape for this kind of dead sprint. I couldn't keep that blistering pace up. Already, my hips burned, and my legs felt jellified. Pain like a needle in my side threatened to drop me to the rough path under my feet.

It got worse. Roots veined the path like the backs of old men's hands. Fred kept going, crushing them down with his heavy tread. I tried to follow in his footsteps instead of navigating what amounted to the Under jungle's version of an obstacle course. It worked at first. Just as I thought I'd made it past the rooty section, my toe caught, and I went flying. I tucked my head and hands, not wanting to injure them or my neck. The last thing I needed in the Under was getting too hurt to use my only weapon, music.

My right shoulder hit the ground at the same time as my right knee. I'd stuck the latter out at the last second. A gritty pain coupled with a pop and threw in the sound of tearing fabric as a bonus. I knew I'd shredded my jeans and done a number on my knee. I sat up, reaching for my bag to get out the instrument I should have thought to use before running. Stupid, I thought. Isn't music, especially mine, supposed to soothe savage beasts?

As I fumbled at the latches on the violin case, I saw nothing but the empty path back the way I'd come. I refused to contemplate why, just continued getting my instrument out, socking it under my chin, taking up my bow. Heavy breathing nearby made me turn to look in the opposite direction. Fred stood with his hands on his thighs, shoulders shaking as he heaved with his mouth closed, clearly trying not to lose his earlier snack. It looked like he'd either hurl or bolt away, possibly off the path. I couldn't let him do either.

I set my fingers on the fret, drew my bow across the strings, drawing out the opening notes of the first song to pop into my head. It took the first verse and chorus before Fred's eyes widened. His hands moved from thighs to cover his mouth, the heaving transformed into muffled laughter. I stopped playing when I got to the bridge because Fred didn't need the music anymore, and by then, I felt ridiculous. I set the violin in my lap and laid the bow on it.

"Seriously?" Fred chuckled. "You won't play *Free Bird*, but you'll play *Welcome to the Jungle*?"

"Seriously?" I answered his chuckle with a smirk. "You won't say thanks, but you will give me grief about rescuing the cookies you almost tossed?" I winced before I could tell him what Grandpa would say in Russian about rude friends.

"Crap on a crap cracker, Irina." Fred hunkered down next to me. "Why didn't you say anything?" He reached out, almost touching my knee but stopping short. I studied his face. "You busted yourself up good.

"Yeah, so what?" I shrugged. "At least I can still play."

"But how are you going to walk?"

"What do you mean?" After the initial burst of pain, all I'd felt from my knee was numbness. I looked down, then looked away again immediately. "Oh."

My knee wasn't round anymore. There wasn't much blood, but the whole thing looked crumpled, as though my kneecap had been the front end of a car and the path a telephone pole.

"Okay, then." I squared my shoulders, staring directly at the path so I wouldn't have to look Fred in the eye. "I'm not going to walk. You keep on going. Leave Daryl's sticky note with me, and I'll use it to call for help."

"No farking way." Fred's jaw was squarer than my shoulders. Square. Root. I tried not to let hysterics take over as my brain went along mathematical pathways to cubes and exponents. I had to be in shock.

"Well, you can't let me set the pace. Ed needs you on a deadline."

"Normally, I'd just use some magic to heal you, but I'm low from all the upchucking and Spite friendliness."

"You can fix this?" I waved at the knee I couldn't look at.

"Yeah. But not when I'm like this." He rubbed his belly. Well, it wasn't very belly-like, more like a solid wall of muscle. Toned muscle. I wanted to hug him. I felt my eyebrows try to shake hands. I never noticed things like that. Had to be the pain, or maybe whatever had made me think a saber-toothed tiger-horse was chasing me.

"In case you haven't noticed, I've stopped your hurliness twice already." I raised my instrument again, resting my chin on it. "Let me help you help me."

"Guess it's worth a shot." Fred smiled with his big, sharp teeth. I smiled back. "Hope you can keep playing through a snack and what I'm going to have to do to your knee."

There was no way I'd ask him what he meant by that, especially since time had us under more pressure than Freddie Mercury and David Bowie ever sang about. Also, the pain and I had become fast frenemies without the "fr" part. I took a deep breath and drew my bow across the strings. Brahms Lullaby slid out as instinctive as the old hair metal song had minutes earlier. I needed something to soothe, and that was the piece Grandpa had used to chase my nightmares away after we only had each other left. If that old tune couldn't keep Fred and me calm and focused, nothing would.

Memories of Grandpa flooded my mind from just after we'd stopped that battle from becoming a war. The older lines of sadness etched into his face joined by-products of fresher grief that mingled with time. I thought of him, wondering how his physical therapy had gone, whether he'd end up coming home, only to hear I'd been lost in the Under. But of course, he'd hear about Fred and Ed, too. He'd understand more than anyone else I knew why I'd come here. How much of a sucker I was about helping people in danger, especially this particular kind.

Fred wiped his mouth. I wondered why I smelled pizza, and sure enough, there were three boxes from Caserta's tumbled in a heap to Fred's left. His bag had to be magic, then. I'd suspected, but it was definitely bigger on the inside.

Our eyes met. That morning, they'd been a flinty blue. Here in the Under, they glowed red. Either way, they held the same warm concern. Fred's true self, revealed by the faerie realm, was more than just Redcap teeth, giant size, and changes in skin color. The man had the body of a monster, but a kindness that dwarfed his form, in direct opposition to any assumption his appearance might be likely to inspire in most people.

"I'm sorry, but this is going to hurt." He put his hands on my leg, one above the knee and the other at the shin. It tingled. I closed my eyes, continuing to play the lullaby. He waited. I felt the tingling increase, then ebb away like a diminuendo.

A pop, louder than the one when I hit the dirt, sounded through the jungle as though all that foliage hadn't been able to absorb the sound. When I breathed in, I smelled salt. My bow skidded across the strings, ending the lullaby with a screech.

I screamed. Something solid kept me from falling over before I passed out.

CHAPTER NINE

Fred

When Irina screamed, I knew she'd fall unconscious. I did the only decent thing and caught her, then turned my head to the side as I lost the rest of the pizza. I didn't know why losing my cap affected me that way. All I knew was Redcaps weren't as powerful without it. I'd never taken it off, either. Not since the first time my magic made itself known. I'd been three and eaten half my train set. Poor Mama.

After wiping my mouth on the napkins I'd taken out for that purpose, I took the violin and bow from Irina and put them in the case. Then, I gently turned Irina on her side. The knee still had shallow scrapes, but I'd knitted the fragments of her kneecap together with my magic and then relocated it with plain old elbow grease. I wasn't sure Irina knew how badly she'd been hurt. If she didn't, I wasn't going to tell her unless she asked.

I brought the thermos out of my bag and wet a fresh napkin, then dabbed her face with it. We'd have to get moving. While the scrapes would sting and she'd be a little achy, we could still get through the strange mood-altering jungle. Those flowers, the enticing scent, had to be the reason she'd taken off like a contender at the start of the Boston Marathon. It hadn't affected me, but maybe it was a trap to get mortals off the path. Irina moved her head, groaning as she wiggled her leg. Then, she opened her eyes. She closed them again almost immediately.

"Where'd the trees go?"

"Huh?" I looked up. Irina was right, there weren't any trees. Instead of a jungle, we sat at the grassy beginning of a wide beach edging a turquoise body of water. I sniffed the air. "Salty. I don't remember anyone mentioning the Sidhe queen having an ocean."

"Do many of the folks you run with mention her at all and actually know what they're talking about?" Irina turned to lay on her back, staring up at me.

"Good point." I nodded.

"I've heard of this." She sighed. "It's not an ocean exactly, but a gulf."

"Okay."

"You're not going to ask where I heard it?" Irina moved her leg again, bending the knee a little. A little, relieved sigh escaped her lips.

"Nope." I shrugged. "You'll tell me if you want to."

"Most people pry like I'm an oyster with a giant pearl inside." She sat up. "You're weird, Fred."

"Back at you, Irina." I winked.

"It's a good thing." She grinned.

"Agreed." I smiled because, so far, she hadn't seemed to mind, even with my full-on Redcap looks. Usually, that kind of thing scared everyone away. Well, besides the others in Tinfoil Hat, but that's the way it is with packs led by wolf shifters. "Anyway, we should go look for the path again."

"Isn't it just going to go along the beach and around the gulf?" Irina got up, brushing grit off her hands and shaking it out of her hair.

"Not necessarily." I pointed at the sand. "You see the path, right?"

"Um." Irina squinted, tilted her head, shrugged. "I give up." She closed her violin case and tucked it back in her satchel.

"Look again." I kept pointing, moving my finger closer to one edge of the path we still occupied the middle of.

"Oh!" She clapped her hands once. "I see it now. It's like all the sand is, I don't know, moving the same direction? Casting a different shadow? Anyway, now I can't unsee it."

"Good." I got up, brushing sand off my hands, then the seat of my pants. I ignored the puddle of sick from earlier, turning my back to it.

"Anyway, thanks for helping with the knee." Irina settled her bag on her shoulder. "Let's go."

We did. The dry sand made it hard to walk, but there was no way either of us would take off our shoes. Boots are cumbersome, heavy, and leaving them behind was out of the question since we didn't know what other terrains we might come across. When the path got closer to the water and became damp sand, I almost breathed a sigh of relief. It led beside the water, not so close we'd get drenched. The way it curved wasn't parallel to the shoreline, though. I had no idea how this path could lead to the queen's castle if it, as we'd seen through the sprite's lamp, were on dry land.

Up ahead was a pier. I could tell by the curve that was where we had to go. When we got to it, the path continued along the weathered wood to where a small boat floated, moored with a thin gray rope. Peering out over the water revealed no sign of a shore on the horizon.

"Well, this sucks." Irina pointed into the dinghy. "No oars."

"Guess we're up Seelie Creek without a paddle." I scratched my head. "Hey, didn't you say one of those sticky notes said Pixie on it?"

"Yeah," Irina grinned. "Just the thing for water, right?"

"Exactly." I pulled two yellow squares apart, glancing at them. Then I put the one marked Imp in my pocket and used the other to summon a Pixie.

I wasn't sure what to expect since I hadn't actually seen a Pixie of the water variety before. When an inky black splotch in the water resolved itself into a vaguely humanoid shape, I blinked and stifled a laugh. brownies were sticks. I expected Pixies to be fish-like. But when their blue-green head surfaced, I thought they looked more like a Gnome but less squat and barrel-chested. The Pixie wore a toga made out of some kind of scaly hide, silver and gray like a salmon's. They kipped out of the water, landing on the boat's prow like a gymnast planting. They even held their little arms up in a vee.

"Hi!" They waved like a pageant contestant on a parade float then hooked one thumb at themself. "My name's Nixie. What's yours?"

Irina doubled over, laughing so hard I thought she'd fall head-first off the pier and into the water. I reached out, ready to catch her in case she did, but she managed to control herself.

"Please," Irina gasped, "whatever you do, don't start singing *Let Me Entertain You* from Gypsy."

"Aww." Nixie pouted. "You ruined my fun. Just a tiny bit." The Pixie grinned, putting their first finger and thumb so close together they almost touched.

"A Pixie who knows musicals?" I chuckled. "Who'd have thought?"

"You see something new every day." Irina shook her head, cradling one side of her face in her hand. "So, Nixie, I assume you can pilot this boat."

"I can do that!" They winked. "And a mean tap routine to go with it."

"As long as it gets the boat across that gulf while staying on the path, it's all good." I winked back at Nixie, then climbed carefully into the boat.

Irina's achy knee gave her some trouble, so I just lifted her and placed her in the stern. I wasn't sure why she stared at me for the next couple of minutes after that, but I tried not to let it get to me even if it made me feel funny. I turned to face Nixie, wondering why my face felt all fever-hot.

"You're forgetting something, mister." Nixie pointed at the worn brass cleat.

"Oh, yeah." I reached around but mucked up the knot with my fat fingers.

"I got it." Irina swatted my hands away and had it undone in seconds.

"Okay!" Nixie clapped their hands, and the boat set off, either via some magical invisible force or current under the water moving it, possibly a little of both.

The Pixie, true to their word, tapped out a dance along the gunwales as we went. I bobbed my head to the rhythm of their feet, trying to figure out the familiar beat. And I definitely recognized the sound of metal clasps unhinging. I couldn't be surprised that a girl who'd chosen music over magic would want to make some during an impromptu performance regardless of the strange surroundings.

"*Singing In The Rain!*" With accompaniment, I finally recognized the routine Nixie danced.

I sang along, of course. When we all performed together, I could have sworn the boat moved faster. After the song had ended, the current slowed. I scratched my head.

"What's with the speed change, Nixie?"

"Didn't you know?" They smiled. "Pixie magic works better in groups. Actually, most Seelie magic does, for us pure types, especially."

"I never knew that." I nodded. "But it makes sense."

"How so?" Irina had set her violin in her lap in order to rub rosin on her bow.

"Seelie faeries are all about following rules. Any kind will do."

I gestured at Nixie, then Irina's violin. "It'd make sense that when more of them do the same thing at the same time, they're stronger." I held up the end of the old rope that had tied the dinghy to the dock. "It's like this rope. Lots of strands in here, all contributing to making the boat stay put."

"So wouldn't it work that way for Unseelies, too?" Irina put away her rosin.

"Nope." I shook my head. "Unseelie magic bends the rules. It's about improv, and skirts the indefinite."

"Huh." Irina tilted her head and worried her bottom lip. I rummaged in my bag and handed her an unopened tube of Chapstick when I found one. I nodded at her murmured thanks. "It's weird. In the old stories, the king's always seemed a whole lot scarier than the queen, but since the Reveal, it's almost like people think about it the other way around."

"That's because Her Majesty's so absolute." Nixie sighed. "It's been difficult here since the Reveal, because now that humans know the truth about faerie Courts, they tend to prefer the Unseelie side."

"Wow." I blinked. "Nixie, I'm sorry. We've been sitting here ragging on your queen while you've been helping us."

"Don't worry about it." The Pixie shrugged. "You're still a changeling and your bard's carrying Her Majesty's favor. Also, I know why you're here, Fred Redford. For what it's worth, I wish we were meeting under different circumstances." Nixie smiled like they stood on a Broadway stage instead of the side of a rowboat. "Anyway, how about another musical number?"

"You don't have to ask me twice!" Irina socked her violin under her chin and took up her bow. "I'll start this time."

Irina struck up a tune that I'd never have recognized if Mama hadn't been a closet fan of old musicals. Nixie jumped for joy before launching right into the dance number. I tossed all sense of dignity to the wind as I belted out *All That Jazz* from *Chicago*. It felt odd to sing about rouging my knees and rolling my stockings down, but I couldn't come up with a more manly alternative to the original lyrics.

"Wow, I can't believe you actually sang that one, Fred," Irina smirked.

"I can't either." I winked. Her knee had to be feeling better because more than enough color came into her cheeks. "But it was worth it. Look!" I pointed.

"Yay, land!" Nixie clapped their hands. "Shall we do another?"

Before I could answer, something dragged along the bottom of the boat.

"Um, are we over a sandbar or something?" Irina's eyes flicked from side to side.

"No…" Nixie's eyes widened. "Get down!"

Irina did, but I couldn't hide in a boat that size. And that was why I saw the tentacle before she did.

"Hey, Irina! Play something, would you?" I bared my teeth. "Calamari! Just like Mama makes!"

I waited for my musical cue, then took a bite out of the cobalt-blue appendage. My teeth clamped down. Cold blood, nothing like marinara coating my tongue. Sure, Redcaps could eat anything, but we rarely wanted to. Still, this overgrown squingini salad was attacking my boat and my friends, trying to stop me from rescuing my brother. Where in the world did it think it was, at an audition for *20,000 Leagues Under The Sea*?

I opened my jaws and bit again, deeper this time, knowing by feel that I'd come closer to severing the squid's limb. It let go with that one, but another reared out of the water. I chomped that one, too. As long as Irina kept playing, I could defend the boat with nothing but fists and teeth. And I could tell by the tippy tap of little feet that Nixie was doing everything they could to keep the boat moving along on course.

The tune pouring from Irina's violin was *A Little Priest* from *Sweeney Todd*. I couldn't believe the first thing that came to her mind at a time like this was cannibalism.

"I'm not a squid, dammit," I shouted between bites.

"Sorry!" She kept on playing. Once the chorus ended, she switched over to *Le Poisson* from *The Little Mermaid*.

"Better!" I kept on biting and fighting, pushing twitchy tentacle ends out of the boat as I went.

Nixie danced up a storm and the boat moved on, dragging whatever Under version of a squid attacking us along with it. I wondered why I wasn't tiring or getting sick, even without my cap. I thought I should have at least been feeling run down. Instead, it seemed like I could do this for hours. I looked down, finding my hands tinged blue with blood or ink or whatever, unsure whether one squid or many harried us. When I looked up again, I could see the pier.

"Land ho!" Nixie had one hand over their eyes, sighting our destination. The Pixie jumped, clicking its heels together.

Irina tilted her bow, beginning another song. Just as I recognized the opening notes of a song from *The Pirates of Penzance*, she screamed. I turned my head and made a grab right along with her, but both of us were too late. Her bow hung just out of reach, suckered on to one of the tentacles. I reached out and up, trying to wrestle it, but the boat rocked, precarious like a car on an icy mountain road. I sat back down.

Nixie kept on tapping as Irina plucked strings. It was enough to power the boat but not steel my gut. I swallowed, trying to keep the wannabe squid sashimi down until I could at least get my head over the side of the boat. I managed, but just barely.

Once the creature got Irina's bow, it let us go. Irina put her violin back in its case, shaking her head as she gazed at the empty spot where the bow went under. The little dinghy coasted up to the pier, and Irina tied it off. I stayed for a moment, splashing water to wash my face and hands, hoping there wouldn't be any reverse encores of my impromptu dinner. Once my stomach settled down, I got out.

"Sorry, but this is where I exit stage left." Nixie smiled gently this time. "If you're ever on this side of the Under again, look me up. I'd love to perform with the two of you again."

"Thanks, Nixie." Irina held out a finger to the Pixie. It actually shook with her. "Likewise, if you're topside."

Nixie gave me a salute, then dove into the gulf. I watched them vanish, a receding splotch against all that blue water. I turned back to the path and trudged on, Irina following along in glum silence.

CHAPTER TEN

Irina

I walked along slightly behind Fred for the second time during this whole crazy journey. I didn't want him to notice how down I'd gotten about losing that bow. It wasn't even the original one Grandpa had from back during WWII, but still. Without it, my limited power in the Under shrank to almost nothing. Sure, I could pluck, but that limited my song choices and didn't seem as powerful, judging by the end of the squid fight. Maybe my pride in being able to play anything on a violin had taken an inevitable fall. But this was the worst possible time for that to happen.

I kicked small pebbles and rocks along the path, not daring to chase any that went off to the side. One of them hit Fred in the ankle, and he turned around to stand like a barricade in my way.

"Listen, we're almost there." He tapped one foot. But feet that big can't really tap. More like thudded. "I'm sorry for bringing you here. You've suffered from this whole trip more than I have."

"Wait, what are you talking about?" I blinked up at him. "I banged up a knee and lost a bow. You're the one forcing himself to eat and puking his guts out every time we run into trouble.

And don't pretend you didn't get all ominous about losing your cap. Just because you think your pal Tony stole it for a good reason doesn't eliminate the consequences for you if you don't get it back soon."

"Hey, if there's a bright side, then who's got two thumbs and is gonna look on it?" Fred jerked both his thumbs at his chest. "This guy." After that, he shrugged. But this time, his easy, amiable smile went absent. "Everyone has a crutch."

"Crutch or not, we need to face the facts here." I put my hands on my hips. "I mean, listen to yourself. You come in here dead-set on the idea that you'll never get back home. How are you even sane? Unless you're lying about it."

"You may be right. I may be crazy." This time, one corner of his mouth turned up. But I knew that song.

"I'd rather look for a lunatic than a liar. So tell me now, which is it?" This time, I tapped my foot.

"I'm not lying." That ghost of a grin on Fred's face vanished. "And you owe me now."

"What?" My eyes widened as I stared at him. His behavior made no sense like he really had lost some of his marbles. Or maybe biting the squid monster had mood-altering side-effects.

"Careful, or you'll owe me more." Fred actually tittered. It sounded like thumbtacks hitting corrugated tin. "You just asked me three questions during the same conversation."

"I thought that only applied to tithed and pure faeries."

"Normally it does, but this is the Under. And I've already helped you three times." His eyes glittered, that red color in them coming on stronger.

"Fine. Great. I owe you." I smiled in the face of Fred's attempt at intimidation. "But you know, I don't mind. I'll be happy to get you and Ed out of whatever mess this is. Maybe you won't have to stay here, except for the regular year and a day tithing time."

"You can't do that." Fred closed his eyes, looking wearier than

I'd ever seen him. "No one and nothing can do that unless I get my cap back."

"Since I'm already in the hole with you, Fred, I have to know if this is right. It has to be your cap, not just any cap."

"Has to be mine." He nodded. "Our caps aren't like Selkie and Kelpie pelts. They can't be passed on."

"Oh. Well, that sucks." I stepped closer to him so he'd get the message. Fred Redford couldn't scare me off for my own good or any other reason. "So, like I said before, I owe you. I'm sure you have something in mind."

"Yeah." His gaze bored into mine. "You're going to tell me exactly why you're helping me."

"That sounds like a waste of a favor."

"It's not." His glare intensified. "You don't know Ed or me from Adam. You know an awful lot about Seelie stuff. Tony didn't take my cap to give to the queen, but some boy-toy of hers is out hunting it down, anyway. You went on about a jinx and denied the existence of the Extramagus, who I know has been messing with my friends for over five months. That crazy bastard targets pairs. I thought the duo he's hating on this time is my brother and me because nothing else adds up. So, what if you're his pawn, or even worse, his ally?"

"I don't get it." I did, but he looked so focused on his theory, I didn't think it possible to distract him from it.

"Tell me why you came to the Under, Irina." Fred bared his teeth, his red eyes gleaming with a light that looked less than sane. "Tell me now. And if it turns out you're working for the douchecanoe who's been offing people, I'll make like the shark in that Internet meme who eats faces."

I glared right back at him, wishing I also had glowing eyes. My Empathy kicked up, making me want to turn it around and attack him. With the Psychic power making me psycho, I couldn't just close my eyes and take a deep breath, either. I felt everything he did at that moment. His anguish, rage, confusion, all wadded up around a core of anxiety and inadequacy. Fred's optimism, while genuine, was just one layer. Only the debt and the question he'd asked in payment stopped him from treating me like an enemy. I'd had no idea how frayed his self-control had gotten during our journey, but now I shared it because that was just my flavor of Psychic. Luckily, I also got that thin leash of faerie custom. It was more than enough to rein me in.

"Fine." My hands clenched into fists, nails digging into my palms. It brought some semblance of myself back from Fred's emotional turmoil. "What's happening to Ed almost happened to me. The difference is, the queen never managed to get me into the Under."

"How?"

"Because my parents were Psychic and also changelings. That was why they waited so long to have me. They held off until I was old enough not to need both of them all the time because they tithed opposite Courts."

"Who even does that?" Fred blinked.

"A couple who thought they could change ages of Monarchal ill-will with their love. They'd both had the same vision, something about how examples of love prevailing would shift coincidence and reunite the king and queen. And it didn't, of course."

"So, where are they now?"

"I'll get to that. When the queen tried to convince me to go with her, my father said no. She went to strike him down, and my mom got in the way. She pushed him out of the way. They were forbidden from touching, of course, after they tithed. And when they did, it almost started a war right in the middle of Providence. Ask your dad about it sometime. He was there. You could ask Sparky, too. The poor Sprite got captured in that battle, trying to help me get away."

"So, why wasn't there a war?"

"Me and Grandpa. We stopped it from getting worse by playing." I patted the violin case at my hip. "Our music calmed everyone down and stopped the fighting, but it was too late for Mom. Someone hit her with an iron bar, and she died of her injuries."

"And your dad?" Fred didn't blink, but the gleam in his eye got less baleful, more watery.

"The queen executed him for the crime of embracing an Unseelie Courtier. He gave her one last kiss before she died, you see."

"She killed him for that?" Fred shook his head, nostrils flaring.

"Yeah. And he was one of her knights, too." I felt exhausted, more tired than after that mad dash through the jungle.

"Oh, Irina." Fred's shoulders dropped. "I had no idea. No wonder you chose music."

"At least I had a choice."

"Because you're not a changeling?"

"That's right, not a bit of it. Took after Grandpa almost exactly. He stuck up for a whole camp full of people he didn't know when he was younger than I am now. And his history plus that battle, what happened to my folks, that's why we've only got each other. And it's why I won't stand by and let the queen pull this bull with another family. It doesn't matter that I only met you today, or I don't know Ed at all. I know what you're going through, what could happen. That's enough reason for me. Never again is the Kazynski way, you know."

"I'm so sorry." Fred hung his head, turning it away, so I only saw his profile. "And so grateful you still think I deserve your help."

"It's okay." I reached out, pausing before patting his shoulder to check his emotional state. He felt deflated but not defeated. My story hadn't broken him, just busted a big hole in the suspicion he'd built, that his deteriorating sanity had directed at me. I changed my hand's trajectory and brushed his cheek with my fingertips. "I'm an Empath. Telling you I understand is an understatement."

"Thanks." Fred closed his hand over mine. When he looked back at me, all the rage had eased, replaced by gritty determination. It was like a breaking fever, except emotional. He stepped to the side and faced forward, still holding my hand. "Now, look above the trees and tell me what you see."

"Towers." I barked out a laugh. "The castle already!"

"Yup." Fred squeezed my hand gently. "Now, nothing's standing in our way."

I knew that was only more brash optimism. Fred still had no cap, leaving him at risk for another episode like this one. I could barely play my instrument. But I wouldn't correct him because I couldn't be sure I wasn't wrong. After all, we still had one more sticky note, and the mountain of conviction between us seemed higher than the wall we'd toppled earlier in our Quest.

We walked along the path, the thicker trees giving way to parkland. The full castle came into view, and even though the clock chimed ten, we knew we'd make it in plenty of time. It only took about five minutes to see our error in judgment.

The castle had looked peaceful at a distance, and it was easy to imagine it mostly deserted and protected by wards. On closer inspection, the place was crawling with guards armed to the literal and figurative teeth—brightly armored Sidhe, trolls manning catapults, brownies poised in crossbows with helmets like spearheads, djinn waving curved blades, and Spites in spiked collars patrolling everywhere.

"So, what do we do now?" Fred scratched his head. "Summon the last of the sticky psychic paper crew?"

"I think that's probably our only option." I glanced down at the slightly smudged ink. "It's an Imp. I'm not sure how one of them can help us."

"Do you know what Imps do?" Fred shrugged. "I'm not sure."

"Do you know Gnomes?" I handed the paper to him.

"Yeah." Fred rolled his eyes. "Ornery, sneaky, and powerful.

Loyal when they actually find someone they like keeping around."

"Imps are kind of like less surly Gnomes, only Seelie. They look a bit different too, but there are some extra things you should know before we call one for help. You know the story of Rumpelstiltskin?"

"Who doesn't?" Fred cracked his knuckles. "What a jerk."

"Okay. Well, that story must have been inspired by an Imp."

"So they're miracle workers?"

"Yeah, you could say that." I sighed. "They have hearts like mercenaries, though. They work miracles for a price."

"Ugh." Fred made a face like he'd bitten a lemon. "No chance we could guess its name?"

"That's one part of the story that isn't true." I shook my head.

"Oh." Fred paused, holding the note gingerly. "So, what exactly can they do?"

"That's really something you should ask the imp." I shrugged. "I only know they seem to do impossible things."

"Yeah. Well. You only rescue your little brother from the Under once, right?"

"Right." I cleared my throat. "Well, you do. And we hope we don't have to do it again even though nature loves a sequel."

He used the paper. A rush of displaced air brushed my sleeve, along with a pop. We turned to greet the wizened little person.

"Hello. I take it you need a miracle?" The imp grinned, twirling the end of what looked like a beard but turned out to be a hairy triangular scarf.

"You could say that." Fred looked distinctly unimpressed. "All the same, I'm not sure you'll be able to deliver on this one. It's a pretty tall order."

"Manners, lunk." I elbowed Fred, then leaned down and held out one hand. "I'm Irina—"

"Yes, yes. You're the Kazynski girl. And the big fellow there must be Fred Redford. Good to make your acquaintance." They grinned. "Daryl told me all about you."

"Wait, what?" I blinked. "How?"

"Oh, they told me in the future, you see. After everything that'll happen later on, of course." The imp shrugged. "You can call me Ziggy. The two of you have many talents, but naming things is not among them, so I've taken the liberty. Now, tell me what you need."

"Okay, Ziggy." Fred held up one hand with the fingers curled down. He raised one for each item. "My cap. A bow for Irina's violin. Something to help us neutralize the army guarding that castle over there. And a partridge in a pear tree."

"I can do all of those things." Their entire face crinkled when they smiled.

"The partridge in the pear tree isn't a requirement, of course." I rolled my eyes at Fred. "That one was a joke, you know."

"All the same, I can give him everything he asked for with enough time to spare."

"No way!" Fred took a step back.

"Way." Ziggy laughed. "I believe in miracles. When I'm done, so will you."

"But I don't even know where to find any of those things, or even what one of them is." Fred narrowed his eyes.

"I do." The imp smirked.

"I can't possibly imagine how." Fred shook his head.

"I'm an imp." Ziggy giggled. Their laugh was creepy instead of charming like the Pixies'. "We have our methods, but you may not like our prices."

"Okay." Fred crossed his arms. "So lay the price thing on me then, miracle-worker."

"In the future, you'll see me again. You'll also be given a choice to condemn or give mercy." Ziggy smiled slyly. "Give it."

"I can't imagine that being a price he won't like." I bit my lip, trying to figure out the downside of this deal. "I mean, you seem to know something about Fred. You must already be aware that he's the merciful type."

"It's not going to be as easy as it sounds when the day comes." Ziggy sighed. "Miracles aren't cheap, even when they're easy. Having mercy at that point in time will be costlier than it seems now. And you're right; this is a tall order, but I can do it. Give the word if you can accept these terms, Fred Redford."

"I accept."

"Great." Ziggy smiled. Their teeth looked like crystal or maybe cut glass. I wondered whether they might have replaced them like Gnomes or if that was just how an Imp's teeth always looked. They tugged on that beardish scarf and vanished with another pop.

"Are you sure that was a good idea?" I raised an eyebrow.

"No, but what else could I do?" Fred shrugged.

"You could have just asked for the cap and the bow, I guess." I sighed. "The thing to stop an army is probably what makes that request such a doozy. Or, you could have haggled a little."

"Maybe, but an act of mercy seems a fair enough price for a miracle." Fred stared up at one of the towers. "And it's not even mine, it's for my brother."

I sighed, hoping I wouldn't have any "I told you so" moments with Fred later. I was about to thank him for adding a bow in with his requests when a third pop signaled Ziggy's return. This time, the rush of air that came with them was much bigger, blowing my hair all around my head and into my face. I pushed my hair back to see that the imp had brought company.

"Lane!" Fred's exclamation identified the vaguely familiar long-haired fellow standing next to Ziggy.

"Um, hi." Lane glanced from Fred to me and then back to Ziggy. "What gives, little dude? I was just minding my own business, and here I am at—" He glanced up at the heavily defended castle. "Okay, where in fang hill are we?"

"The Under, Lane. A long walk outside the Sidhe queen's

castle." Fred glanced at the guitar bag slung over Lane's shoulder. "Thank goodness you have your guitar. I understand why Ziggy here brought you. Music. That's got to be the solution to one of my problems." He turned to face the imp. "This is only one item on the miracle list, buddy."

"Oh, I assure you, Mr. Meyer has everything with him you need to complete your Quest." Ziggy chuckled. "But I've almost forgotten something. Here's the last item."

The imp waved their hand, and we had to jump out of the way as the earth at our feet cracked. A sprout wove its way up and out, growing faster than Jack's beanstalk from the stories. The scent of blossoms gave way to a fruity aroma as green globes mellowed to gold amongst the leaves on the new tree. I blinked, then gasped when I heard a chirp and warble. Up at the top, a partridge perched. When we looked around, Ziggy had gone.

"But we're missing two things," Fred groaned in frustration. "Why did I have to trust that imp?"

"Um, Fred?" Lane unzipped his guitar bag and pulled something long out of it.

"My spare bow!" I squealed when I saw the ruddy wood and tawny hair. "Where did you get that?"

"From a friend." Lane handed it over. "It all makes sense now, why he gave that to me."

"Whatever. You're a lifesaver." I opened my violin case and began rubbing the horsehair down with rosin. "Thanks."

"Don't mention it." Until he smiled, I'd had no idea Fred's friend was a vampire.

"So, who should I thank for having the foresight to get you my bow?" I smiled back. Vamp fangs were no big deal to me anymore.

"Tony. He stopped at your grandpa's house to finish Fred's job and then met me at the band's practice space."

"Wait." Fred scratched his head. "I thought Tony was the one out running around, keeping my cap away from the Extramagus."

"No." Lane reached into his back pocket. "Tony just stole your cap at the party. I don't know where he got his information, but he knew we had to get it before someone else did. And he wasn't the one running around with it the whole time. That was me, or at least until dawn, it was." He held something slightly squashed and red out to Fred.

"You?" Fred sniffled, turning his head away from his friend. I could see the tears standing in his eyes, even if Lane couldn't. "But the Pack thinks the Extramagus has Fire magic. You took a risk like that—for me?"

"It was nothing really, dude." He hid it well, but I could tell Lane was lying through his dainty little fangs. I stepped back to give the buddies the space I knew they'd need.

"Didn't I just say last night that you sound like a surfer when you say dude, bro?" Fred punched Lane's arm.

"And you sound like a meathead when you say bro, mofo." Lane jabbed Fred in the ribs.

"Hipster." Fred clapped Lane's shoulder and didn't let go.

"Sick burn." Lane mirrored Fred's gesture.

"Spectral Magus."

I watched the bro-est of bromantic hugs ever to happen in front of the Sidhe Queen's castle. Letting them do their thing would take a couple of minutes, but we were early enough according to the clock on the lowest of the castle towers. And anyway, the good vibes were exactly what all three of us needed. I'd been nearly exhausted and close to hopeless before. All that changed even more drastically than the sun coming out after a thunderstorm. And to think, it was all thanks to an imp and a couple of vampires.

CHAPTER ELEVEN

Fred

"So, Lane." Irina gave him a sideways glance. "What exactly do you do besides being of the nocturnal and fangy sort?"

"I sing and play guitar in a lame band in Providence." Lane took one look at Irina's violin and went all googly-eyed. "Oh. My. God! Is that a Stradivarius? Tell me I actually just saw a Stradivarius in person!" He jumped up and down like Mama always said she used to at Duran Duran concerts.

"Yeah, you are," Irina grinned, picking up her instrument to show it off. "It's my grandpa's."

Lane didn't spare a glance at the king's and queen's crests inside the case. Of course, faerie anything was more than a little outside his realm of experience. I realized that with all the goobing, fanboying, and fangirling over the rare violin, Lane hadn't answered Irina's question. She didn't want to know whether he was in a band, she'd been asking about his extrahuman powers.

"Lane's a garden-variety vampire, as far as magic or Psychic stuff goes." I cleared my throat to be sure they paid attention, glad they'd lent me an ear each so I didn't have to repeat myself.

"He was just a regular guy who happened to be an up-and-coming front man when he was turned."

"Oh?" Irina tilted her head. "That's odd. No offense, Lane, but most vampires don't bother turning anyone nowadays who doesn't have some other mojo besides music."

"It's a long, strange story." Lane shook his head. "Probably best to save it for another time. Anyway, Fred, you said music solved one of your problems already?" Lane peered at the castle walls. "I think maybe you're a little out of it after being separated from your cap for so long."

"Nope, not a bit of it," I grinned. "Irina here has been doing all kinds of things with her music to help us get this far. Playing together just enhances the effects. I think, if we all work together, we can give them an encore they won't forget here on the queen's side of the Under."

"And would you mind filling me in on why you're storming the Sidhe queen's castle before you lay anything else on me, bro?" Lane rolled his eyes, but he was grinning, so I knew it was all an act.

"Sure thing, buddy." I told him about Ed and the queen's ultimatum. It took a while because I didn't want to leave out any details.

"Woah." Lane shook his head, flipping his long hair over one shoulder. It was blue this week. "Okay, so music. How do you think it's going to help against armed guards?"

"Because I'm Psychic. An Empath, to be exact." Irina slipped the violin under her chin and pointed at a group of guards with her bow. "I project whatever feeling we want at them until they give in to it. How about we play them a little something to help them sleep?"

"Yeah, okay." Lane nodded and unslung his guitar bag. "Just no *Free Bird.*"

"What is it with you guys and *Free Bird?*" I chuckled. "I mean, am I the only person in the world who likes Lynrd Skynrd?"

"No, you're not." Irina sighed. "Look, everybody likes them."

"Yeah, and that's the whole problem." Lane snorted. "I swear it's the most frequently requested song, like, *ever*. That's why we don't wanna play it. It's older-school than our dragon librarian."

"Fair enough." I shrugged. "So, how about *Stairway To Heaven?*"

The collective groaning had harmonic appeal, even with my own voice added in. Yes, I groaned at my own terrible joke. Lane had been used to it for years. I wished Irina could have been, too.

"I really don't know what's going to put all the queen's dudes to sleep," said Lane, "but I know what works for you. Since you're the closest thing to them, being a changeling and all, maybe we should play that one."

"Wait." Irina giggled. "There's a specific song that actually puts this lunk to sleep?"

"Huh," Lane grinned. "Lunk. I like that insult. Can I borrow it?" He raised an eyebrow, and she nodded.

"Wait just a minute, Lane." I shook my head. "There aren't any songs you play that make me sleepy."

"That you know of!" Lane threw back his head and did his evil villain imitation cackle. He turned so I couldn't see the front of his guitar, then put his fingers on the fretboard a half-dozen times.

Irina snickered, then made similar motions on her violin's neck. I shifted my weight from one foot to the other, wondering what they communicated about in their weird music-related form of sign language. Lane was my best friend, and Irina had one of the best reasons ever to go on a quest in the Under. They couldn't possibly be thinking of doing anything to hurt me or ruin our chances of rescuing Ed, could they? I shook off the paranoia, finding it way easier than I had just ten minutes earlier because I had my cap back.

The queen's territory had been nice and warm the whole way, but I still shivered when familiar notes emanated from the two instruments. It was that same Beatles song Night Creatures performed at Josh's party, Golden Slumbers. My eyes widened, watching ripples rising up from the guitar and violin, like heat shimmer over asphalt in the summertime. Irina stared right at the manifestations of her Psychic powers, so I knew I didn't imagine them. She pursed her lips, and the ripples flew away from her and Lane, bridging the gap between the castle guards and us.

But something was missing. I waited for Lane to start singing. He was one of the most talked-about local vocalists in Providence, after all. But all they did was vamp. I'm not talking about the extrahuman kind, but the repeat of intro bars like a holding pattern as the instrumentalists wait for the vocalist. And that's when I understood that Lane wasn't going to sing. They waited for me.

I did my best, fully aware that I was no Paul McCartney. But being in the Under and having my cap, knowing that two famously talented musicians who happened to be my friends had my back made all the difference. Even though I'd sung already on this adventure, it'd been like a parody, mimicry, something to do just so I could be useful. This was as different from that as rehearsal is from performance.

When I opened my mouth, I didn't find my voice. It found me, like that moment at an airport when a friend spots you first after they've spent years abroad. I'd knocked the rust off my voice, the one thing I'd given up on years before to prepare for taking over Redford Renovations someday. I let that part of myself make its way across time and distance to find me again, and I welcomed it with open arms.

My mouth formed words about ways to get back home, singing a lullaby. And the guards, all those pure and tithed faeries, stopped their glares and glowers. Their eyelids drooped along with their shoulders. They put down their weapons, leaned in doorways and on battlements. I saw an imp curl up at the feet of a brownie and a Spite snuggle against a troll. All the pure Seelie creatures I'd heard about in bedtime stories meant to scare me into behaving fell asleep to our music. We defeated the monsters from my childhood without striking a blow, overcoming them with a peace they'd left themselves vulnerable to instead of the war they'd prepared for.

And we advanced. I went first, walking along as I sang. Lane and Irina flanked me, though there was no need for the defensive formation. Everyone and everything slept. I peered at the armor, weapons, insignia as we passed unchallenged all the way up to and through the castle gates. Faeries of all ranks had fallen to Irina's sleepy Empathy. I wondered for a moment why I wasn't also tired, then turned my head to glance at her. A separate psychic shimmer hovered between Irina and me, her and Lane, too. She was the one keeping me awake. I wondered where she got the energy for all this Empathic projection, especially since she'd given up on that the same as I'd done with singing.

And that's when it hit me. Mama was Psychic, too. She'd even told me a bit about it. She never got tired when using her power for something she believed in or the people she cared about. I'd been right to trust Irina. She was in this with her whole heart, not just along for the ride or because of some superstition about a jinx. Not even for honor's sake or revenge for her parents.

I kept on singing, repeating the short verse and chorus over and over as we moved through the castle, searching for that courtyard Sparky had shown us. We didn't even have to talk strategy or stop the music to agree on which direction to try next. Our course of action was just there, a fact agreed on between us like we were linked.

I felt like nothing could stop the three of us.

CHAPTER TWELVE

Irina

Our music echoed, the acoustics everywhere in the queen's castle nearly perfect. The only thing tired were my feet. I focused all the raw desire for peace, home, and sleep coming through Lane's guitar, Grandpa's violin, Fred's voice. My eyes misted with unshed tears. Home was something I'd considered to be a place free from as much Extrahuman influence as possible, a negative space. But when I'd plunged headfirst into this venture because, yet again, the queen decided to mess with a kid, I realized a void, no matter how vast it might seem, couldn't be home.

The magical world was a part of me, regardless of whether I'd thought myself a part of it. I couldn't get rid of my powers in all this time. In fact, I'd used them to gain popularity, enough money to get by. My tears weren't for Fred, his brother, or even Grandpa. They were mine, for my life so far and the new possibilities for my future.

Telling Fred the story of my parents had wrecked me as much as I thought it would. The immediacy of our troubles had helped me stave it off. But now, evoking emotion in everyone around us,

I had to acknowledge my own. I'd self-injured in a metaphorical sense, cut part of myself off, not denying it, but using it. How could I stand up to the queen, defy her for exploiting a child, when I did the same to my own scapegoated talent?

That doubtful seed grew in my heart, irony stopping me from squashing it dead. I'd been a coward, a fake, and worse than that, a hypocrite. How had I been this blind for four years? Who was I to walk in here, the queen's home, when I didn't even have a place to belong for myself?

A voice, almost mine, interrogated and harried me mercilessly. I was nothing, a hollow persona people clicked "like" for on the Internet because I manipulated them with a power I claimed to hate. My music moved them, moved us through these stone halls, because of my Psychic power, not my musical talent. I was a fraud, unworthy of Grandpa's respect as a musician or a descendant. I'd run away at Water Place park the second the djinn's shield went down.

The emotions, the internal monolog, the tears, all those came from my heart and mind and body. But they didn't speak with my words or in my voice. The speaker was the impostor, not me. And that's because the one stirring the roiling pot of old trauma wasn't me at all. Someone else in this castle was awake.

I told that other Psychic to take a flying leap at the moon. All that time, I'd only lied to myself, set myself adrift, wounded myself. No one else got hurt because I'd been a pathetic mess. And I had to be honest, finally. What kid who knew her parents died for her mistake wouldn't be wrecked? And what was wrong with that, anyway? Grief is natural.

When it counted, I'd come back to Providence. I helped Grandpa when he needed me. I'd been contemplating having to stay in Rhode Island, even though it wasn't what I wanted, ready to do it because I loved him. And when I heard about Ed, the queen's ultimatum, I'd stepped up even though I didn't know the Redfords and feared faerie anything.

I grinned, let those threatening tears make good on their promise to soak my face, kept on playing *Golden Slumbers*. And I wasn't surprised when Lane played the classic Beatles medley changes to finally segue into *Carry That Weight*, or when Fred's voice moved on from pleading with a sleepless darling to sending invitations.

The quality of the sound told me more than my bleary eyes did. I knew we'd turn one more corner and reach the courtyard. But when we did, I wasn't prepared for what we saw there.

The round stone table was nearly full, twelve seats occupied by fierce faeries armed to the teeth with emblems and colors that marked them all as knights in the queen's court. A mix of Sidhe, trolls, djinn, and even a Goblin sat there, a more diverse group than I'd imagined here on the Seelie side. Their armor varied in amount and type of wear, some looked dinged and scarred from battle while others gleamed with a high polish. Besides being knights, these faeries had nothing in common. No, they had one other thing. All twelve dangerous looking warriors were awake.

The queen waited on her throne, sitting up this time instead of crosswise as she had in the vision from the Sprite in the lamp. Her foot tapped in time to our music, and she stared intently at me. I'd heard the Goblin King was a Magus also, one who could use several schools. Was the Sidhe Queen Psychic in a similar way? Could it have been her voice I'd heard in my head, trying to convince me I was worthless? That would have been enough to make me hate her, but the fact that she probably had an inherent talent for percussion just made it even worse. My cheeks flushed so much they felt sunburned.

Fred sang the words to *Ending*, staring at the kid perched on the dais at the queen's feet. Ed. I glanced at the wall behind the throne, over the queen's head. The hands pointed at twelve. We'd found him in time. But had we actually spent a whole hour navigating the castle? No way. Fred sang the last notes, words about how love taken equals love made, which tapered off as the sounds from our instruments faded.

One person's applause echoed around the courtyard, but no one had their hands up, at least, not that I could see. Fred made a blind spot between me and the door. I stood still, bow arm at rest, and waited to follow Fred's lead when it came. But Lane looked around. He had a better view back the way we'd come than I did.

The vampire stepped back, tumbling into Fred as he hissed like a feral cat. If he hadn't had a strap, his guitar would have clattered to the flagstones. As it was, he busted an E string. I saw it hit his arm and break skin. At least he hadn't bled all over the place. Vampires generally didn't unless they'd just fed. I shuddered, hoping Lane wasn't hungry.

Lane held his hands up to his eyes and crawled into Fred's shadow. He huddled there, smoking slightly. The flannel shirt tied around his waist had caught fire, and his long blue hair was singed at the ends. I pulled the shirt off his waist and stomped out the smoldering cotton, knowing the undead vampire would end up plain old dead if that went up. Then, I dared to peek around Fred's massive bulk.

A tall, thin man in a pale-yellow suit was leaning on a cane that looked to be more for fashion than balance. Or maybe it was a weapon, like those sword canes. He looked older than us, maybe in his late forties, and as handsome as a model. He seemed familiar, especially once I noticed the graying blond hair under the black-banded straw sun hat he wore. I couldn't place where I knew him from, though. It wasn't easy to look at him either because his hat didn't block the sun. Instead, what looked like sunlight emanated from under it, his hands, too.

"A Spectral Magus?" Fred scratched the back of his neck. I'd gotten so used to him scratching his head, but understood that couldn't have felt normal from his perspective. "Thought you said the last thing you needed was sunshine, Lane."

"Yeah. Sick burn." Lane mumbled with his head bent over his guitar as he restrung the E. He had to be even more dedicated to music than I was, doing something like that after nearly going up in flames.

"Epic vampire reflexes, Lane."

"That's what she said, Fred."

"Ew, d-bag central." I stared right at the Magus when I said it this time, instead of down my nose at Fred and Lane. He deserved it.

"What would you have me do with these miscreants, Your Majesty?" The Magus did all the down-nose-looking I hadn't at the guys as he gave the queen a half-bow. Even though he clearly answered to the queen, I got the impression he had way less restraint than any of us.

"Wait," she said simply. She looked anything but simple, sitting there in her ornate robes with the delicately crafted crown tucked amongst complex braids in her amber hair. "I still have negotiations to attempt. And turn that light off, Richard."

"Yes, Your Majesty." He bowed again, and the light under his hat and around his hands dimmed. Just as I thought his magic had gone back to normal, it darkened instead. I blinked. Was this what Fred meant by an Extramagus, a person who could use more than one kind of magic? I'd just seen him using Spectral, and now it looked like Umbral. For some reason, that rang a bell and felt familiar the same way his appearance had. I didn't know why. It bothered me, so I reached out with my Empathy toward this Richard person, trying to sense anything I could from him.

I managed to just lower my violin instead of staggering back. The sheer force of his ambition shamed me as my own desire for YouTube fame wilted like a flower in the desert of comparison to his aspirations. It wasn't just ambition either, but lust for power, for domination, for his vision of the world. It was like the inverse of my own. I craved surroundings without magic. He wanted nothing less than the subjugation and eventual annihilation of everything non-magical. And that's where I knew him from, why he was so familiar. I knew all about the kind of man he was. Grandpa used to tell me stories of guys like this Richard. The moral in all of them was to do anything within your power to stop those people from coming to power.

This megalomaniac was the queen's ally, a close one. After his magical display, I understood why she'd want him to be. He was powerful, versatile, talented. But his sanity felt like a frayed bit of cloth unfit for even dusting Grandpa's knick-knacks. I wondered how she couldn't know this about him. She had to since he was here in her throne room, and I suspected she was Psychic. What good was being the Sidhe queen, ruler of half the Under and close to half the faeries, if she couldn't sense a madman when facing one. She had to know, right?

As he approached the throne to stand at its left, my eyes widened. I blinked to keep them from bugging out. She snapped her fingers, conjuring a stool out of thin air. He sat on it, and she held her gloved left hand toward him. He bent and fawned over it, looking at her with that fire of lust in his eyes. And I knew it wasn't the sexy-times kind of lust, either. He wanted her power, to be a partner to it at best or use it at worst. Some of those stories Grandpa told had been about the faerie courts, how a seat at the left of the throne was reserved for a consort.

I glanced at Fred. His jaw clenched so tightly that his teeth squeaked as he stared at the display of ersatz affection between Richard and the queen. Ed gazed up at him, his head tilted, but Fred wasn't looking his way. Ed caught my eye instead. I wished I could mentally wipe off my Empathy before reaching out to the kid with it, but that's just not how it works. I had to reassure myself with the idea that Ed had been seeing something like this for at least part of the time he'd been here already.

Ed felt nervous, worried about Fred. It made sense, considering how I thought he'd been convinced to come here. But when his eyes widened in surprise as he studied my face, I knew something else was going on here. Didn't Fred say his mother was a medium, that the queen had taken Ed because he was one, too? The Under had ghosts, people who'd died here. Was he listening to one right then? What could they be saying?

Ed swallowed, glancing sideways at the queen and then the empty space to his right where I thought the ghost was. I opened my mouth to ask the kid what was going on, almost forgetting where I was and the situation we were in. Ed held up a finger, but it was more his sudden pang of fear that made me shut my trap.

"Frederick Redford, stand forward." The queen's words cut through the silence like glare through vision. "Alone."

"Yes, Your Majesty." Fred squared his shoulders to leave Lane and me, standing like the base of a pyramid suddenly robbed of its apex.

CHAPTER THIRTEEN

Fred

I stood before the Sidhe queen, chin tilted up and shoulders back. It's how I was raised to behave in the presence of royalty, with the expectation that I'd tithe to a different Monarch someday. The king liked his subjects to display courage and confidence, so that's what I did here.

I didn't care one bit that she expected bowing, scraping, or courtly fawning. Anyway, Ed wasn't doing any of those things. I wouldn't either. Richard the yellow-suited dandy seemed to have plenty of that to spare, anyway.

"Do you have anything to say for yourself, changeling?" The queen's eyebrow raise was Major League compared to any I'd seen out of Lynn Frampton, though Blaine's mom might have given the queen a run for her money. Maybe that was why those two were friends.

"Yeah," I grinned. "I'm here to collect my brother, your Majesty, just like it says in your letter."

"And what do you think of my side of the Under? Its denizens?"

"Piece of cake." I didn't go so far as to wink at her though her weird question made me want to default to nervous joking. So I elaborated so she wouldn't think I'd just insulted her domain. I actually liked most of it, jerk teenage brownies and squid monsters aside. "Which is to say, it looks good and smells good, but doesn't do a body good if you take too big a bite out of it with the wrong kind of appetite."

"Well, it's decision time for you and your dear brother, then." The queen waved her hand, and I heard a sound like a twig snapping.

Ed blinked. Then, he smiled. He stuck one foot out, then the other, shaking them. I knew these mannerisms of his, the ones he always used when listening to a ghost's story for too long and his feet fell asleep. My brother got up, walking like a cat on a freshly mopped floor. He came to stand by me, striking a miniature imitation of my own pose with one exception.

Ed's head was almost always tilted to one side or another, a side-effect of his Psychic ability. I imagined Mama used to be that way when she was a kid, too. Then only other Medium I knew, Bianca, only did it sometimes, and she was halfway between their ages at least. Ed always listened for ghosts. He had to. Unlike faerie glamour, Blaine's magic dragon sight, or Maddie's Umbral hiding spells, Ed's Psychic powers to see and hear ghosts couldn't be turned off. It was like he saw twice as many people as anyone else in the room with him. The same thing went for Henry with his memory sensing Psychic ability. If he touched the wrong thing, it was memory lane time, whether he wanted to take a trip down it or not.

I didn't glance back at Irina but wondered whether it was the same way for her. I wished I could talk to her just then, ask her what the queen might be planning. But I hadn't expected a quiet conversation in the throne room, asking questions or making decisions, and especially not Ed standing right next to me. Even with my cap back, my stomach churned and rumbled like a cement mixer. Everything was nerves for me during that thirteenth hour.

But then a wave of calm came over me. I knew it wasn't mine. No words came through, but I got the impression of a slight smile in a pale face, an angular fall of dark hair across a forehead, distant strings playing that old classical lullaby from the illusory jungle. Irina. She'd just used her Empathy to calm me down so I could face the queen without screwing things up. After that, I remembered every word in the queen's letter. A decision wasn't mapped out in her original bargain.

"Well, I'm not sure there is any decision for me and Ed to make, your Majesty." I pulled the crumpled letter out of my pocket and held it out. "It says I have until the clock strikes thirteen to collect my brother. I'd say that's happened already, so we're square. Now, it's been real, and it's been fun. But Mama's going nuts without her boys at home, so if it's all the same to you, we'll be leaving now, Your Majesty." I gave her a nod instead of the bow she probably wanted, but I didn't care. I'd treat her the way I'd been taught to treat the king. If she didn't like how I behaved in her throne room, she shouldn't have stolen my brother and dared me to confront her in it.

"Um, Fred?" Ed's voice wasn't as tiny as I thought it'd be.

"What's up, small fry?"

"My letter was different." My stomach sank as Ed rustled an enchanted paper from his own pocket. "It says, if I want to go home, we have to come to an agreement." He unfolded it, and I read it. My face felt redder than my cap.

"He's just a kid, Your Majesty. You can't be serious about holding him to this."

"If I weren't serious about it, I wouldn't have written it with my hand or sent it with my magic." The queen raised an eyebrow opposite the corner of her mouth that tilted up in a half-grin. "In the future, whichever of you accepts my offer will do well to phrase such ideas as questions."

"What does she mean, Fred?" Lane either had brass balls or a death wish. Or maybe he was under the impression he had nothing left to lose.

"This letter of Ed's is a contract. It says someone from our family will serve the queen or Dad's getting exchanged for one of the king's friends in the queen's dungeon." I shook my head. "I understand why you signed this, Ed. But I can't let you honor it. Mama would kill me and then bind my ghost to work at a garbage dump for a hundred years."

"But I can't let you honor it either, Fred." Ed glanced off to the side at whatever ghost he'd befriended here. "He says it's a bad idea. He took one like it years ago, and it ended up leaving his daughter without any parents."

"But that's only because he broke his oath." The queen smirked, her eyebrow lowering. "Both of you know better than to do something like that."

"Wait a minute. What, exactly, did he do?" I peered at the spot Ed had been listening to.

"Held his wife as she lay dying, Fred." Irina's voice carried a note of inflammatory irony I hadn't expected from her. Of course, being in front of the queen would be difficult for her, but I'd assumed sadness would win over anger. "I think we should huddle up here."

Ed, Lane, Irina, and I made a square in the middle of the space before the dais.

"That ghost. It's your father."

"Yes." She hissed the word. "Don't take the deal, Fred. She'll just try to find a way to kill you."

"But if Ed serves her, he'll never be able to come home from the Under." I sighed, suddenly weary for the first time since I'd set foot in the queen's demesne. "He'll be a kid forever. He'll never see Mama or Dad or me again. I can't let that happen to my family. Not when I can serve here for a year and a day, then come back Seelie. Sure, I have to avoid my father, but Mama and Ed will still have him, each other, and they'll be able to visit me wherever I end up living. And I can still talk on the phone with Dad. It's a no-brainer, really."

"And probably exactly what Her Majesty wants, too. It's like she wanted Fred tithing to her all along. The stuff in your way getting here wasn't even all that bad compared to what it could have been. Almost like they were tests to see if you'd fit in here." Lane's comments made me remember just how good he was at putting things together when stakes were high, and he actually paid attention. "Look, I gotta disagree with the siren of the Stradivarius here. I think you should take the deal, Fred. You're an engineer, do crazy math in your head all the time. Rules are more your thing than not. You might even do well, going Seelie. Besides, if the queen wants you serving her so bad she pulled shenanigans like this, you could drive a much harder bargain than what she's offering."

"You want him to haggle with her?" Irina shook her head, blinking at Lane. "For what?"

"I dunno. I'm not a changeling, just a vampire. And some of the older ones sure do like their negotiations. It's just what my gut says—that you can make a better deal with faeries—but I don't know how. Thought maybe one of you might have ideas." He grinned at me.

"None." I sighed.

"What about the empty seat at the table, Fred?" For once, Ed wasn't looking at an invisible-to-me person. "That's her round table of knights, and it looks like she's missing one. Why would anybody want to go through being a page and then a squire when he could start off as a knight?"

"Well, you know what they say." I glanced over my shoulder at Richard, the queen's creepy suitor. "Once a king, always a king. Once a knight is enough."

"What does that even mean?" Ed asked Lane because he knew I wasn't telling him.

"You can hear the other meaning when you're old enough to understand it, kid," Lane grinned. "Basically, it means everyone remembers kings even when they get deposed fast, and especially when they make a mess of things. But it's enough for some people to just do heroic deeds and be a good example."

"Seriously?" Ed eyed my friend suspiciously. "Or are you making fun of me again, Lane?"

"Seriously. And I have to say, your brother Fred's hands-down the best good example I've ever met." He clapped me on the shoulder with one cold hand. "He already knows I'm gonna miss him. You shouldn't be stuck here forever without that example, squirt. I'll try to pass on what I learned from him while he's gone for a year."

"And a day," I added with a sniffle. Somehow, knowing Lane would be there to give advice to my kid brother comforted me, even though he was a blood-drinking vampire.

"Hey, me too." Irina hooked her bow on her belt and ruffled Ed's hair. "I'll be right down Rochambeau if you need anything. I'll have to stay in town to take care of Grandpa, anyway. And hey, maybe you'd like to learn to play." She gestured at her violin.

I turned to look at Irina and Ed. She didn't even know the kid, but their shared experience of almost being stolen away to faerie bonded them. I could feel it through the Empathy she projected between all four of us.

"One other thing I think you should ask for, Fred." Ed looked back at me. "This ghost who's been helping me."

"Wait, what?" Lane did a double-take. "I thought ghosts of people who died in the Under couldn't leave."

"That's just because they're usually tithed and die with unfinished business." Ed gestured back over his shoulder. "This ghost's never going to finish his. If I bring him up, at least he can be around people he cares about."

"Is it really my father?" It was Irina's turn to sniffle. She peered at the spot Ed had gestured toward. I knew she was feeling something about the ghost through Ed's mediumship, even though she couldn't see or hear him.

"Yeah, that's your dad." Ed made a wistful grin. "I don't want to leave him stuck here."

"Okay, I'll ask for his release then, too." I nodded. "We done?"

I waited for everyone else to nod. After that, I turned around and stepped forward. A glance at the clock told me we still had maybe a minute before the clock struck thirteen.

"Your Majesty, we've come to a decision."

"And?"

"We're leaning toward the idea of my staying here for a year and a day, tithed in service to Your Majesty. But we have some terms to discuss." I pointed at the empty seat at the round table. "I see you have no Redcap knights. That chair's been empty so long it's got cobwebs. If I tithe to you, I expect to occupy that seat immediately, and I accept with the duties and responsibilities that go with it. That's my request, Majesty, but I'm not the only one you made a contract with today. Ed has his own terms for you to hear."

"Your Majesty, I'd like to start by thanking you for your hospitality." Ed smiled. Irina gasped. Creepy Richard froze in the middle of his fawning. My kid brother had unexpectedly courtly game. "I want to help Sir Fred when his year and a day is done." His grin changed over to the grave face he always made when he pulled one over on Mama. "But I need to know more about your rules, and there's no one to teach me. I'd like you to release your bond on the ghost of Samuel Kazynski so he can come home with me as a tutor in all things Seelie."

I didn't have to look back at Lane to imagine his smug grin or the thumbs-up he had to be making at Ed. The clock's hands clicked over to thirteen. I held my breath.

"Done." The queen's voice had the first chime of that fateful hour for accompaniment. In the space between that and the next, I put one hand over my heart and bowed to Irina, touching the hand that held her bow to my forehead. On the third, I walked to the table, pulled out the empty chair, and sat. Lane nodded at me on the fourth chime. Irina gave me a salute with her bow at the fifth. Ed wiped his eyes when the clock chimed six, his hair moving in a nonexistent breeze that could only be the ghost of Samuel Kazynski trying to help comfort him.

Six more chimes sounded, allowing me to lock eyes and drink in my friends' faces one more time. When the clock struck twelve, the queen snapped her fingers. I blinked. When I opened my eyes again, the knight to my right, a Sidhe I vaguely recognized from school, had vanished along with my brother and my friends. The thirteenth chime began my first day tithed in service to the Sidhe queen. But I figured if my voice coming back felt that good, a year and a day in the Under might not be so bad. And I already had a reputation for using it.

Irina

I couldn't see a thing, so I didn't move. I shook with anger, though. Had the queen sent us into some black hole or pit where she could forget about us forever? After I opened my mouth, but before I could scream, someone's phone beeped, then said, "Verizon Wireless."

"Signal, yes!" Lane's voice came from somewhere to my left.

"Does that mean we're not in the Under anymore, Toto?" I still didn't dare move.

"Yes. We've been transported out." I didn't recognize the voice, but it was male with a refined lilt to it, coming from somewhere in front of me. I knew the queen wouldn't send Fred back until it'd been a year and a day, but the fact that she'd apparently sent along a lackey had me fuming.

"And who's this?"

"Oh, that's Sir Al," Ed piped up from my right. "He goes to school with Fred."

"Hello," said Al.

"Like that's supposed to tell me anything. I don't go to PPC, remember?" I started to roll my eyes but stopped when I realized no one else could see either. Well, except for Lane. Vampires could see in the dark. "Lane, where are we?"

"Oh, sorry." Off to my left, plastic clicked as a switch flipped.

I still couldn't see a thing, blinded by the sudden glare of bright lights. After rubbing my eyes with my forearm, I looked around. We stood in a square windowless room, decorated with posters of electric guitars. Thick rugs blanketed the floor, foam egg-crate covered the walls, and tapestries hung from most of the ceiling. A drum set squatted in one corner.

"Oh, wow!" Ed ran over to the big bass drum, tracing the NC painted on the front. "I'm in the room where you guys practice." He grinned. "So cool!"

"The queen was supposed to send us home, I thought." I raised an eyebrow as Lane went to the mini-fridge in the corner and got himself a bag of blood.

"She couldn't since our friend the vampire hasn't been invited into the right houses." Sir Al adjusted the stiff collar on the long pale-gray jacket he wore.

"But he comes over to our place with Fred all the time," Ed almost whined. I couldn't blame him. It'd been a long day.

"Ah, but technically, Fred's no longer a resident there. And I can't be at your house with your father at home." Sir Al took a pair of glasses out of a pocket and put them on.

Lane wiped his mouth and tossed the empty blood bag in the trash. All his burn injuries had healed.

"Did the queen send you here to lecture us or for some other reason?" I probably shouldn't have been so surly to this Sir Al guy when I didn't even know him, but I missed Fred already.

"She sent me to make sure you're all home safe." He leaned against the wall, then stood up straight again once he squished into the foam. Al turned to look at me. "And also to extend you an offer, Irina Kazynski."

"Wait, what?" I blinked, realizing I'd have to cool it with the questions.

"Her Majesty would like to invite you back some time to visit Fred during his year and a day." Al turned his head, and I noticed his long ponytail of nearly white hair. "Ed, as well."

"What am I, undead chopped liver?" Lane sighed.

"Unfortunately, in a manner of speaking, you are." Al grimaced. "I'm sorry. The queen's more than a bit biased against anyone nocturnal. Besides, I don't think it's safe for you with the queen's new suitor there."

"Wait a minute." I felt bad for Lane, but this was good news for Ed, at least. "Now I'm confused. I understand extending invitations and all—keep Fred happy, let Ed learn more about the Seelie court. But something doesn't make sense. She's inviting me, a faerie nobody?"

"Did you not understand what Sir Fred did before taking his seat at the table?"

"Um, no." I remembered him bowing to me and taking my hand, but I didn't want to talk about it. I'd decided to just keep that moment to myself, hope that he'd come looking for me the day he came out of the Under.

"Faerie knights serve a monarch. We take on the Quests they assign us, tasks to help the demesne prosper. This is similar to what pages and squires do, but knights have certain privileges. We get to choose our strategies, play to our strengths, and dedicate our heroic deeds to someone we admire. Sir Fred chose you, Irina."

"But why would he do a thing like that with his best friend and his brother standing right there?" I blinked, the back of my hand tingling as though it remembered the feel of his.

"You'll have to ask him yourself." Al inclined his head. "You'll both be able to visit in a month if you'd like."

"You must have dedicated your deeds too, Al." Ed's smile was over-the-top sweet, so I knew he must have had an ulterior motive for asking.

"That's another privilege of knighthood." Al's small smile was slier than a fox's. "We can make our choice on the matter private. Unlike me, Sir Fred made his dedication in perhaps the most public way possible."

"Yeah. Sounds like my brother, all right." Ed shrugged. "Anyway, I have to go home. Mama's going to have a fit."

"I'd go with you, kid." Lane sighed. "But there's still too much sun out there."

"It's okay." I packed my violin and bow. "I'll go with him and explain everything."

"Yeah." Lane mumbled something about undead chopped liver again as I walked out the door of the practice space with Ed in tow. Al followed us out.

"One other thing." The Sidhe knight stopped us before we got even a few steps away from the old converted mill.

"Okay."

"I wasn't sure how to tell this to Mr. Meyer without betraying my monarch, but I do not trust the queen's suitor, Richard." Al glanced at Ed, then me.

"I don't blame you." Despite the summery temperature out on the street, I shivered. "I'm an Empath. He's just about the creepiest dude I've ever been around."

"Yeah, Samuel doesn't like him, either." Ed cocked his head, presumably toward my father's ghost.

"I've got a touch of precognition in my family background." Al glanced around before speaking again. "I saw something bad in store for Lane Meyer in the near future, an event which has something to do with Richard."

"Oh, boy." I shivered again. "I don't know how in the world I can help Lane against a guy with Spectral magic."

"But some other people do." Ed tugged my sleeve. "Come on, Irina. And you too, Al, even though you'll have to wait across the street for a while." The boy grinned. "When I get home, I'll use Fred's emergency backup phone to make some calls. It's time for you guys to talk to the Tinfoil Hat Pack. Lane, too. I'll tell him about Richard myself. He'll just think I overheard something."

Even though I didn't know who Tinfoil Hat was, exactly, if they were anywhere near as determined and brave as Fred, I knew I'd get along with them. I looked around at the sunlit streets of the neighborhood I thought I'd left for good. I wasn't stuck here taking care of Grandpa, I was remembering where I came from and giving back. Like my music and my Empathy, this city and the friends I made here would always be a part of me.

EPILOGUE

Ed

It was after eight that night when I sat with my feet dangling an inch off the floor on a booth seat at East Side Pockets. The falafel sandwich tasted awesome, but it only made me miss Fred more. Understanding why he'd tithed to the queen, knowing he couldn't see Dad or set foot in our house again, just made it worse.

I listened to the entire group of college students at the next table, glad they didn't think I'd be paying attention. But I definitely was. If I had any information they didn't, I'd have to speak up. That Richard was worse news than any of them could imagine. Except, maybe, for Irina. She knew. I sent all the thoughts and feelings her dad's ghost had about him right at her. And I just had to hope she wasn't in denial about it. I shook off my own thoughts and listened in more closely. Being a kid had advantages in that department. The attention span one, not so much.

"So, the Extramagus' name is Richard." Blaine Harcourt frowned from inside a smoky haze.

"That's familiar." Lynn Frampton doodled on a notepad. Her

writing was so messy, it was no wonder she wanted to be a doctor.

"Asking LORA now." Kimiko tapped on her tablet, then brushed away paper plates and napkins to set it in the middle of the table where everyone could see. "Ooh, see? He's a Fire Magus. We looked at his registry records before."

"But he looks an awful lot like an old student of Grandpa's." Irina scratched her head just like Fred always did. "Except that's not the right last name. Also, he wasn't Fire. I remember Grandpa saying he did something with ice."

"Could Richard have a brother?" Maddie pulled on one of her curls as she leaned against Henry. "But no. That doesn't make sense. Why would their parents name both of their sons Richard?"

"Yeah, no brother. Richard's only got one sibling, an estranged sister." The psychic vampire shook his head. "Don't ask me how I know that. It's a weird fragment of something in my mind. The thought is off by itself, like part of a wiped memory."

"You really have to get through that box of stuff you have at the bank already," Blaine smirked and rolled his eyes. "I swear you have more trinkets in your safe deposit box than Mother has rubies in her hoard."

"I'll take it all to Vermont with us after I get it tomorrow." Henry pressed his lips into a thin line. "Stupid banks and their daylight-only hours."

"I know you and Maddie will call us with everything when it's done, Henry." Josh leaned one elbow on the table, peering at the tablet. He reached out and tapped Richard's name. "Look, it's his registry picture. Maybe Sir Al can tell us if this is the same guy hanging out with the queen."

"Simply Albert will do, Mr. Dennison." Al bowed his head at Josh.

"Dude, Mr. Dennison's my dad, simply Albert." Josh snorted. "Just call me Josh, man."

"Are you certain?" Al tilted his head. "As a pack Alpha, you merit the same respect as a member of the queen's peerage."

"I'm sure, Albert." Josh grinned.

"Very well, Josh." Al nodded. "This is, as you say, the same guy."

"Oh, no." Nox Phillips finally got a good look at the picture and stood up. The Selkie was the tallest girl I'd ever seen. "No. That's not right."

"What's wrong?" Josh looked up at his mate.

"Either the registry listing has a mistake, or there's some kind of fraud going on here." She pointed at the tablet. "That man is Headmistress Thurston's ex-husband."

"Must be a mistake." Lane rolled his eyes. "Dude divorces his lady to try to date the Sidhe fricking Queen. I mean, Jerry Springer much?"

"No. It's not a mistake." Lynn stood up, too. "It makes sense. What was it Henry said over inter-session? Something about Headmistress Thurston remembering their old crowd, how her ex-husband was one of them. Blaine said he and Kim overheard his mom and the headmistress talking about a guy named Richard over Spring Break. And Ismail," She nodded at the djinn, "you think he's about the same age as Henry." She grinned at Irina. "When was Richard the ice kid your Grandpa's student?"

"It would have been smack in the middle of the seventies, and he was in elementary school, same time as my parents." Irina put her head in her hands for a moment, then looked up again. "Yeah, I think you're probably right. But there's one other thing to ask a couple of people."

I tried to shrink in my seat as Irina sauntered over and sat next to me. She gave me a smile that made me think of cotton candy wrapped around a brick. I swallowed my mouthful of falafel sandwich, then set the rest of it down on the paper plate in front of me.

"Kid, I need to make sure I didn't just see things back in the

Under." Irina's blue eyes stared directly into what Mama always called my baby browns.

"Okay…" I tried not to blink.

"I thought I saw Richard use both Spectral and Umbral magic back there. Did you?"

"Oh, yeah." I nodded. "Saw him use Fire. He made the queen a pretty flower out of it." I had to get Irina and everyone else to stop paying so much attention to me. I just couldn't handle that many living eyes on me at the same time. "But Al saw even more. Why don't you see what he knows without asking more than two questions?"

Irina got up and went back to her table, a frustrated scowl on her face. Lynn flipped to a blank piece of paper and wrote a list. She made a square next to each entry. She had to be the smartest person at the table, and probably at PPC. Maybe even in all of Providence.

"Here." Lynn handed the pad to Al. "I need this survey done before I start the summer courses I'm taking."

"Oh, no. Summer courses? Seriously?" Bobby looked like someone had just told him there'd be no more candy and ice cream ever again. "Thought we'd be spending our vacation at the beaches on Newport."

"Oh, we will," Lynn grinned, waiting for Al to fill in the boxes. "The coursework is all online." Bobby breathed a huge sigh of relief.

"Yeah, awesome." Lane's shoulders went from tense to relaxed in moments. "I'll want as many of you guys around as possible."

"Wait, what?" Josh side-eyed Lane. "Why? Don't tell me you want to make us all go to that Battle of the Bands you and the rest of Night Creatures try to get into every year." Lane grinned sheepishly at the Alpha's outburst. "Oh, come on. You can't possibly be that scared of the Jack Steele Band, or even the front man's gigantic ego."

"It's not a rival musician he fears, Josh," Al said as he handed the pad back to Lynn. "Mr. Meyer is one of Richard's next targets. He'll need your pack's protection in order to survive."

"Galloping Galen!" Lynn's face went pale as she looked at Al's answers. She leaned against Bobby's shoulder with a sob. "Is there any school of magic Richard doesn't know?"

"Well, this is just absolutely peachy." Lane hung his head, staring at the empty section of the table in front of him. "It's going to be a bitchen summer, isn't it?"

ONE SUMMONER'S TALE

A PROVIDENCE PARANORMAL COLLEGE SHORT STORY

Margot Malone stood outside the old mill building. I watched my Psychic friend mope, not liking it one bit. I opened my mouth, about to spout off a silly song to cheer her up, but it wouldn't have worked. Music in general was what had her so down after all.

Being a Pixie's fun, exciting too. We can go pretty much anywhere regular Seelies can, and lots of places they can't imagine. Traveling through pipes, then popping out and surprising people was incredibly fun. So were all the fringe benefits, like sneaking into people's houses and watching their TVs or getting into movies for free. But like all pure faeries, Psychic Summoners can call me up and try to make a contract with me. I'd been helping Margot in just such a way since she got turned into a vampire. She'd had Daryl even longer.

"Nixie, you don't have to wait with me."

"I know." I patted the Spite sitting at Margot's feet on the head. "Neither does Daryl, but it seems like they feel the same way I do."

"Thanks." She grinned down at us. "Both of you."

"No problem, Boss Lady." I winked at her, but it only deepened her pout. "Are you okay?"

"I will be. I'm a big girl."

"But listen, you don't have to be like the song that says big girls don't cry. You can cry if you want to. You can leave your tears behind."

"It's not really a crying thing, Nixie. More like a puzzle. I'm not liking the picture my pieces are making, especially not when it comes to Night Creatures in general and Lane Meyer in particular."

"So, you want to figure out something about the band in the building?" I hopped from one foot to the other. "They've got bathrooms in there. Let me go check them out for you. I can listen in, and go look in the office for their lease."

I didn't tell her that I also wanted to see if any of the guys in the vampire band would look cute out on a date with Margot. She'd been alone her entire unlife, and I couldn't get the song about the matchmaker making a match out of my head just recently. It seemed practically everyone was pairing off in Providence, Rhode Island.

"It's not like that." She sighed, then leaned forward with her arms on her legs. "I've got information, but the hard part is figuring out how to use it. And what for."

"Okay. Keep talking." I made myself comfortable by leaning against Daryl. Their tail thumped against the dirt under Margot's bench.

"Everybody knows I'm good at getting information, and sometimes people offer me a lot of money or favors if I'll either give it to them or keep it hidden forever. It's hard to decide who to trust except for you, Daryl, and Ziggy."

Margot grinned down at me. She was the nicest Summoner I'd ever met, and considered us pure faeries as friends instead of employees or tools. She knew we had opinions and personalities.

Instead of acting like how we feel about what she'd ask us to do was some kind of inconvenience, she'd compromise. She also never forgets that we're old, even older than her vampire self. Contracts with Margot Malone were always two-sided, letting us ask her for help if we needed it. Other pure faeries I knew kept asking when she'd be strong enough to make a fourth contract, hoping she'd choose them.

"I understand." I reached out to scratch Daryl under the chin.

"Maybe you'll tell me the story behind that understanding, Nixie. Someday."

"Maybe I will." I smiled.

But I knew she wasn't ready to hear it, even if I didn't have a ban against telling anyone until the right time. I thought maybe that time was close. And I don't mean that in a "from my point of view, a thousand years is short" kind of way. But there was one piece that didn't sit well. I had to give her a warning, however vague.

"Margot, this is important." Daryl whuffed, nudging me with his shoulder so I'd get up. He sensed it too, then.

"Hmm." Margot narrowed her eyes, then nodded, an unspoken cue for my next line.

"This." I turned and stood directly in front of Margot. I pointed at her, then hooked a thumb over my shoulder at the building where bands practiced their art. "What you're doing, who you're trying to—" I had to clear my throat and choose my next words carefully. "Connect with."

"But of course, I know Lane Meyer and the Night Creatures are important, Nixie." She smiled. "They're the most popular all-vampire band since the Reveal."

"That's not what I mean." I spread my arms out, hands splayed. She probably thought I was making with the jazz hands instead of dropping hints about how big a mess she'd gotten into. "You're important. Your actions, what you decide to do this summer, and who you do it with."

"That's a nice thing to say, Nixie. But I'm okay, just thinking a little too hard. I don't need a musical number to cheer me up."

"You made a powerful person extremely angry, though." I crossed my arms over my chest. "By helping the Redcap and the bard, I mean."

"That's nothing new." Margot grinned. "Before I got turned, I pissed off the wrong vampire. After that, Brodsky went on the warpath against me, but here I am, okay anyway. I'll handle it like I always do, by keeping calm and carrying on."

"I think you'll need more than that this time, though."

"That's okay." Margot gazed over my head at the old converted mill. "I know I can count on my friends, like you, Nixie. Thanks for the advice."

The wink she dropped let me know she'd gotten the hint… and that there was more to the problem she'd be facing than I could say.

CONNECT WITH THE AUTHOR

Find D.R. Perry Online

Website: https://drperryauthor.com/

Author Central: http://www.amazon.com/-/e/B00O6851HO

Facebook: https://www.facebook.com/drpperry/

Mailing List: https://app.mailerlite.com/webforms/landing/p9i8u6

Twitter: https://twitter.com/DRPerry22